# MOON BEACH MAGIC
*a novel*

Natasha Alexander

ISBN: 0615826695

ISBN-13: 978-0615826691

We're all just walking each other home.

*—Ram Dass*

## ACKNOWLEDGMENTS

I want to thank my family, friends, and fellow authors for their encouragement, support, and good humor during my journey to Moon Beach.

Many thanks, André, for being willing to share our home with Vince, Lizzie, Ernestine, and the other residents of Moon Beach while I've been busy running their lives and pursuing my dream. (And for providing your fabulously nit-picking edits.) This one's for you, with love.

Thank you, Alex, for always believing in my ability to pull this whole thing off. You rock.

To my friends Elaine, Santa, Jane, and Bill: thank you for your insightful comments and suggestions at various stops along the way.

To the online community of writers I've grown to consider friends and colleagues: many thanks to Cathryn Grant, Linda Cassidy Lewis, Dana Mason, and Linda McMann for being supportive and terrific writing role models. Please read their books!

Every writer should be as fortunate as I've been in finding the best critique group in the world. To the talented and creative Sea Quills: thank you, Teri Meadowcroft, Georgia Mullen, Christine Parker, and Charlene Pollano for making my fingers bleed and improving the quality of my writing immensely. Please read their books!

Thank you for reading my book. Please take a minute or two to wriggle your toes in the warm sand of Moon Beach, wherever you may find its magic, and do all you can to protect our beautiful earth from any more environmental damage.

## NOTE TO THE READER

If you've already read *Just Desserts: Greed. Lust. Death. Tiramisu.*, this book may at first glance appear to be a case of déjà vu all over again. It's not.

When I finished writing *Just Desserts*, I knew Vince's life had only just begun. I wanted to tell more of his story, and *Moon Beach Magic* is the result. The first twenty-four chapters of *Moon Beach Magic* incorporate the text and story from *Just Desserts: Greed. Lust. Death. Tiramisu.*, with some tweaks and improvements. So if you've already met Vince, feel free to dive in at Chapter Twenty-Five.

Otherwise, plow right in at the beginning. In either case, enjoy!

# CHAPTER ONE

"GET UP!" TONY shook Vince's shoulders to wake him. "Get up." Tony shook harder, and Vince could smell the garlic on his dad's breath.

Vince opened his eyes. Tony's face was just inches away.

"Get dressed," Tony said. "We're leaving."

Vince had close to thirty years of experience with his dad, enough to do what he was told, even when it involved a seemingly ridiculous demand in the middle of the night. He struggled to pull himself out of his dream as he sat up in bed.

It was 2:18 A.M. By the time Vince had gotten dressed, he was fully awake. He followed his father to the garage.

"You drive," Tony said as he handed him the keys. "I don't see no good in the dark. Head for the Pike. *Fretta.*"

Vince took a hard right at Tony's command, then a left toward the highway.

As Vince headed up the entrance ramp to the New Jersey Turnpike, he heard a boom, an explosion behind him. Black smoke filled the rear view window, and Vince saw flames shooting from his old neighborhood. Tony spat *"buon riddance"* out the side window.

Life, as Vince Fantozzi knew it, had just ended. It was 2:27 A.M.

Somewhere in the Carolinas, Tony told Vince to turn east off Interstate 95 and head toward the ocean. He handed Vince a new driver's license and said, "Here. This is you now."

The license had Vince's picture on it, but he didn't recognize the name. Whatever Tony would give as a reason for the new identity was unlikely to be the truth, so Vince didn't even bother to ask.

Life in Jersey hadn't been that great for Vince, so he wasn't sorry to leave. He'd moved back home when his mother was sick, and he watched her waste away over agonizingly long months. He'd spent hours in the kitchen preparing foods he hoped she could eat. Nothing seemed to help her—not the chemo, not the minestrone, not even the amaretto ricotta pie.

After she died, Vince was ready to move on with his life. But he needed cash. And he made a mistake that cost him dearly.

The wigs had come all the way from South America. How was Vince supposed to know the genuine human hair would still be attached to genuine human heads when the shipment arrived at La Guardia? He'd trusted the wrong guy as a business partner.

Getting out of the wig fiasco required more than a little muscle from some of Tony's friends, and Tony never let Vince forget he owed him. Vince's entire life became devoted to doing whatever Tony wanted.

And that was just the way Tony liked it.

"Turn in here." Tony pointed to an ornate fountain cascading around three concrete dolphins in front of a sign advertising Royal Palm Breeze. He gave Vince a four-digit code to punch into the box at the gate, and the heavy iron gate swung open.

Tony had picked the Royal Palm Breeze community, he said, because he liked the palm trees and the vegetation. That was bunk, and Vince knew it. Tony liked the high brick wall and the gated entrance that kept outsiders outside.

Vince's life was not much different in Royal Palm Breeze than it had been in Jersey. Once a week, he would drive to Walmart with as many twenty dollar bills as Tony decided he'd need for groceries, and that was it. Most days Vince would take the long route home, pull the SUV into the Krispy Kreme drive-through and spend the change on an iced coffee, extra cream and sugar. That small sweet pleasure and his daily run, either through the neighborhood or on a treadmill in the garage, drowning out the mess his life had become with his iPod at full volume, became the high points of Vince's week.

He spent every afternoon preparing Tony's dinner, to be served promptly at 6 P.M.


"No eggs," Tony said firmly, "I don't want no eggs." He settled back in the lounge chair, facing his new 65-inch flat screen TV as he turned up the volume. He spoke loud enough that his voice carried into the kitchen.

Vince put the finishing touches on the frittata, carefully arranging prosciutto and roasted asparagus on top of the glistening yellow pie before putting it back in the oven.

"I don't want no eggs," Tony said again. Vince had

gone to three stores before he found the low cholesterol free-range organic eggs with omega 3 that earlier in the day Tony'd insisted he wanted for dinner.

Vince opened the oven door and looked at the frittata browning under the broiler. Perfect. He slid it onto a platter, garnished it with parsley and cherry tomatoes, and carried it to the table.

"I don't want no eggs."

One of these days, Vince hoped Tony would get what he deserved instead of what he demanded.

Then Shirley and Jack moved in next door, and Vince finally got his wish.

# CHAPTER TWO

SHIRLEY HAD HAD an impressive amount of augmentative surgery in her forty-some years. In case anyone she met was unaware of it, she would bend down in front of them, shake just enough to start jiggling and say, "I don't know why, but men always seem to look at my chest."

Shirley's assets were not lost on either Tony or Vince, though Vince held out very little hope or interest in seeing much more of Shirley than what he'd enjoyed when she first introduced herself in the driveway, bending over to pick a non-existent leaf off the ground. She was wearing a form-fitting tank top with "A Hard Man Is Good to Find" emblazoned on the front.

Shirley's bathroom window was made of the rippled glass blocks that were supposed to blur images to the outside world. When she turned on the ceiling light and stood close to the glass blocks while showering, anyone on the outside could see Shirley's most prominent features clearly. The glass block window faced Tony's breakfast table, and he began savoring Shirley's shower along with his morning espresso.

After a week of watching, Tony invited Shirley and Jack to come for dinner.

Vince spent two days cleaning, making sauces, cleaning, rolling fresh pasta, cleaning, roasting peppers, and making fancy Italian pastries while Tony shouted orders at him.

The doorbell rang at exactly 5:45. Shirley wore a low-cut sundress and she leaned forward as she greeted Tony, jiggling ever so slightly. Vince stayed in the kitchen, stirring sauces and making sure the pasta didn't cook too long. He hadn't cooked for company since his mother died and he was looking forward to the opportunity.

He poured chunky sauce on the pasta and sprinkled pungent cheese over the entire bowl. A twist of the pepper grinder and he tasted it: delicious. He carried the steaming bowl into the dining room and set it on the table between a huge green salad and a basket of crusty bread.

"Okay, folks. Dinner's on." Vince sat down with a sigh of relief. Even Tony wouldn't be able to criticize this meal.

Jack picked up a big jug of red wine and started pouring as everyone passed the food around the table and began eating. Halfway through the bottle, Tony started talking. He told Shirley and Jack he'd been a successful banker in Jersey, that he'd made a killing there. He wanted to retire while he was ahead, he said, while he could enjoy some deep-sea fishing.

This was hogwash and Vince struggled to keep his mouth shut. Whatever "banking" Tony had done was not the kind one reported to the IRS. And while he may indeed have made a killing up north, it was certainly not the kind he was implying to his guests.

Vince got up and brought out a tray of pastries, oozing

with whipped cream and shaved chocolate. Shirley grabbed two without taking her eyes off Tony.

It was close to midnight when Shirley and Jack stood up to leave. Shirley leaned so far over Tony she practically fell out of her sundress. Tony sat on his hands to keep from groping her.

The next day, Shirley took a second shower in the late afternoon. She did a slow motion dance in the water and Tony applauded quietly when she finished.

Over the next couple of weeks, Vince prepared dinner for Shirley and Jack almost every night. Once they went to Shirley and Jack's, but Shirley said she didn't like to cook. The meal she prepared was a testament to her lack of culinary skills.

Jack helped Vince in the kitchen rather than watch Tony and Shirley ogle each other. Jack wasn't much of a talker, and he watched to see how Vince made the pasta, the sauces, those desserts. While Vince cooked, Shirley and Tony would disappear into Tony's bedroom, only emerging when the platters of food were set on the table.

One afternoon Tony seemed on edge, at a loss for words. Vince had never seen his father so uncomfortable. Finally Tony cleared his throat and said, "You gotta go."

"What?" Vince didn't understand.

Tony said it again. "You gotta go."

There was a light tap on the door, and Shirley came in dragging a huge suitcase. She giggled nervously when she saw Vince with his mouth hanging open.

"Here," Tony said. "You gonna need something to get started." Tony pulled a small wad of bills out of his pocket and tossed them to Vince. Shirley frowned when she saw the bills land in Vince's hands. "You too old to be hanging on me all the time anyway. Now get out of here." Tony turned away from Vince and picked up Shirley's suitcase.

Vince stared as Tony and Shirley moved down the hall. His stomach did a somersault when Tony's bedroom door slammed shut.

What the hell was going on? Had Tony just kicked him out of the house? Vince shook his head as if to remove imaginary cobwebs. Then he started moving.

He grabbed an empty plastic trash bag and filled it with some clothes, his running shoes, his toilet kit. It didn't take long. A framed picture of his mother, laughing and healthy looking, sat on the sideboard. He tucked it carefully between his T-shirts and headed for the door.

Jack was sitting at his kitchen table when Vince walked in.

"Hey," said Vince. "How you doing?"

Jack looked at him. "You want the truth?"

Vince nodded.

Jack drained his beer before speaking. "I feel pretty good, as a matter of fact. Shirley's a real piece of work. How about you?" He got two more bottles out of the refrigerator and handed one to Vince.

Vince took a long draught. The sharp cold helped him focus his thoughts. He realized he felt light, lighter than he had in several years.

"Great. I feel great." He was surprised by the truth of his words. He did feel great. "Tony's not all that easy to live with."

Jack nodded toward Vince's belongings. "You can throw that stuff in the front closet. Couch is yours as long as you want it."

They sat together in comfortable silence until it began

to get dark. Shirley had always insisted on taking the leftovers home after dinner at Tony's, so they made a salad and reheated Vince's good sausage lasagna. Dinner without Tony tasted delicious.

Jack looked at his watch and said, "I rarely get a chance to watch, but they're showing reruns of *Murder, She Wrote* at 9 P.M. every weeknight this month."

Vince couldn't believe it. He loved *Murder, She Wrote*! This felt too good to be true. It was too good to be true, and Vince worried through the entire show.

As the credits rolled he asked, "How long do you think Shirley can last over there? Tony's one mean SOB. He's used to me waiting on him hand and foot. And he's lying about rolling in dough. He doesn't have any money. At least none that Shirley'd ever get her hands on."

"He doesn't have any money?" Jack frowned. "When she finds that out, she'll be back here in a heartbeat." He cracked his knuckles.

"And that'd put me back over there with Tony," Vince said.

They both thought hard for a minute.

Vince had learned a few things from his old man, and he sprang into action. He barked orders at Jack, and Jack jumped to follow them.

They didn't have much time. They worked quickly, quietly in the dark. Finally, they loaded Jack's Jeep and headed down the street, headlights dimmed until they turned the corner.

They drove out of Royal Palm Breeze, away from the glass block windows, away from the high wall, the steel gate across the entrance. Already the air smelled fresher.

They heard the boom, the loud explosion behind them.

Billows of smoke filled the rear view window.

Vince glanced at the dashboard clock and smiled. It was 2:27 A.M.

Sweet.

# CHAPTER THREE

FOR THE FIRST couple of weeks after Shirley moved in, Tony and Shirley rarely left the house. They barely came out of Tony's bedroom except to defrost and heat one of Vince's carefully wrapped and labeled dinners. They ate at the kitchen table overlooking what had once been Shirley's shower.

Over time it became painfully apparent that Tony's staying power was not up to the challenges Shirley presented. This realization occurred at the same time the supply of Vince's frozen meals became dangerously low.

Shirley rummaged through the back of the freezer, hoping she'd find gold behind the five pound bag of ice, but there was nothing. No stuffed manicotti, not even any of that creamy tomato sauce with roasted peppers. She slammed the freezer door so hard the boot-shaped magnet of Italy fell to the floor. She left it there. Tony frowned.

"Tony, we gotta get some food. You must be starving." She tried smiling at him, thinking how much she'd like to give that new French restaurant a try.

"We go to the store," Tony announced. He was used to

eating his meals at home, and he liked it that way.

Shirley's smile faded. Her well-honed survival instincts kicked in an instant later and she leaned in toward Tony. "Why don't I go to the store so's you can stay here and relax? Then I'll fix you a nice dinner."

Tony was a shrewd man, and smart enough to realize that if he gave Shirley the car keys and some money, there was a decent chance he'd never see either Shirley or the car again. He shook his head no. "We go together."

Shirley pouted as she followed Tony into the big SUV. Neither of them spoke as Tony drove too fast toward Walmart and swung into a handicap spot near the front entrance. He pulled a handicap placard out of the glove compartment and hooked it over the rear-view mirror.

Shirley pointed at the placard. "What's with the sticker? You're no gimp."

"You wanna walk all the way across the damn parking lot? C'mon. I'm hungry." Tony headed for the door.

They settled on some prepared meals from the deli and Shirley piled a plastic dish high with salad bar items. A picnic table with checked tablecloth, bright paper plates, and beach umbrella stood next to a cooler case loaded with all the necessary ingredients for a summer barbecue. Shirley guessed it was supposed to make eating your own cooking look like fun.

She looked at the barbecue on display. How hard could it be to make that shit? You took some meat and some sauce and slapped it on a bun. She ought to be able to handle that much.

"Oh, Tony! Look how pretty! Tomorrow I'm gonna make you a real Southern dinner." She grabbed a slab of pork from the cooler, tossed a tub of coleslaw, some buns, and a bottle of sauce into the shopping cart.

Tony didn't say anything. He'd been stunned by the variety of ways Shirley could ruin a piece of toast, and he didn't hold out much hope for the barbecue. He wondered where Vince was now.

Back at Royal Palm Breeze they ate their deli lasagna in silence, each of them mourning the demise of Vince's chunky red sauce and creamy filling surrounding his fresh pasta.

The next day Shirley dumped the meat in a crockpot, added a little barbecue sauce, and forgot about it. Hours later, she opened the pot and looked in. When the steam cleared, the bubbling mess looked alive. Small gray chunks of meat headed for the surface as if gasping for breath. She stirred it, then tried a greasy spoonful in hopes of a small miracle. She wondered where Vince was now.

Still, she was hungry and Tony was grumbling for his dinner. Maybe the cole slaw would mask the flavor and the soft buns would soak up the considerable grease in the sauce. She leaned carefully into Tony as she set his plate down, brushing her chest against his shoulder to remind him the kitchen was not where her talents were at their best.

They were both silent as they fought to choke down the barbecue. Tony began to think he might have to learn to cook himself, and the thought terrified him. Shirley thought about how and when she would be able to get to a restaurant for a decent meal.

They both wondered where Vince was now.

After dinner they sat in front of the big TV without talking, Tony punching the remote every few seconds to change channels. When Angela Lansbury's face filled the screen, Tony turned off the set.

"That's it. There's nothing but crap on. I'm going to bed." He headed down the hallway.

It was almost dawn when the pain finally scared Tony enough to wake Shirley, who was snoring peacefully next to him.

"I don't feel so good," he said. "Right here." He patted his chest with both hands and gasped.

# CHAPTER FOUR

"YOU GOT ANY ideas where we might be heading?" Vince asked as Jack sped away from Royal Palm Breeze and toward the highway. "Probably we should have worked this plan out a little better before burning our, ah, bridges behind us."

There was a long pause before Jack answered. "I guess further south, if that's okay with you. I've got a friend runs a guest house in this little town called Moon Beach. I'll give him a call later when we stop for breakfast. It's still the middle of the night."

After a couple of egg sandwiches and some coffee, Vince drove and listened to Jack's end of the phone conversation.

"It's settled," Jack said as he ended the phone call. "We can stay in one of Bernie's cottages, at least for a couple of weeks, maybe more. He and his wife have extra room and can even use some help around the place.

"They've been wanting me to visit ever since—" Jack paused before continuing. "Well, for a long time. It'll be good to see them."

Vince drove over a high bridge spanning one of the coastal waterways. Usually he felt uneasy at this height, like he was about to careen over the guardrail and plummet to the water below. Now, though, Vince felt different as the car rolled along high above the water. He felt light and almost giddy with hope.

He'd stuffed this kind of hope to the back of his mind for so long he felt a stranger to it. He was afraid to let it out, to let it shake itself into some kind of new reality.

For several years, Tony had loomed like a dark cloud in the background. But the farther they drove from Royal Palm Breeze, the smaller that cloud became. Maybe with time it would even disappear. They drove for hours in silence, each man wrapped in his own thoughts, his own cloud.

Jack finally broke the silence. "Turn off the main road up there at the stop sign. We're getting close." A small sign read: Moon Beach - 2 miles.

Vince turned. The secondary road was paved, but just barely. It ran roughly parallel to the water, and occasionally they passed close enough to the bay to see white sand and sparkling water. Then a clump of scrub pine or a small enclave of old trailers and cinderblock cottages would hide the water from their view.

Time slipped backward.

"That must be it." Jack pointed to the weathered sign for Whispering Pines Cottages. "Turn right there."

Vince pulled the Jeep into the long gravel driveway that curved its way through woods, finally stopping at a clearing in front of a house perched high on pilings.

A man watched from the deck above them as they parked. His flip-flops clomped against the wooden steps as he headed down to greet them.

"Jack. My man." Bernie gave Jack a rough bear hug, careful not to spill the olives from his drink. "Long time no see." Bernie took another sip and sucked on an olive. Then he stuck out his right hand and clasped Vince's. "You must be Vince. Well, any friend of Jack's is a friend of mine, especially one who's responsible for finally getting my buddy down here to visit."

Bernie pointed to a cottage almost completely hidden in the woods. "Unload your stuff into Lemonade. It's the big yellow cottage. Then come on back. I'll make some coffee and you can fill me in on life until Anne gets home from work. She can hardly wait to see you."

The Whispering Pines Cottages were set far back from the road, nestled in a thick grove of palms, live oak, waxmyrtle, and hanging vines. There were, as far as Vince could tell, no pines. Lemonade's screen porch seemed to hang in the midst of the woods, and they were able to tuck the car under a canopy of vines.

The Lemonade cottage had two bedrooms, a large bath, and what realtors would call a great room—a kitchen, dining, living room combination. It was furnished with a combination of early Goodwill and late Walmart, and in need of a little sprucing up, maybe some fresh paint.

Out on the deck, Bernie poured both of them steaming coffee, pointed to the sugar and cream pitcher on the table. He looked directly at Jack.

"We have a lot of catching up to do. It's been, what, about a year now?"

Jack stared at his mug for a long minute before answering. "I don't even know where to start." He turned to look at Vince. "My wife was killed by a drunk driver fourteen months ago. Bastard had an open bottle in his hand, cocaine in his system. Drove right up over the sidewalk. He was too drunk to walk when witnesses dragged him out of his car. At least Janet never saw him coming. The only good thing about it."

He sighed before turning back to Bernie. "I was a mess, still am in some ways. I moped around for months, couldn't get my mind on anything. Everywhere I looked, I saw Janet, thought of Janet, needed Janet. Probably would have been easier if I hadn't already retired, if I had something else to focus on.

"Then one day Shirley showed up on the doorstep. Said she was Janet's best friend from way back." Jack shook his head. "I don't remember Janet ever mentioning her, but who knows."

"Anyway, Shirley gave me this song and dance about her husband dying, too, and she had nowhere to go. Blah blah blah. I felt sorry for her. I let her move into the guest room for what I thought would be a couple of weeks."

He shook his head again. "Big mistake. Every time I told her she had to leave she'd break into tears and come up with some story or another about why she couldn't.

"The worst part was Lizzie, though. Shirley insinuated that we were, ah, having a 'relationship.'" Jack put air quotes around the word when he said it.

"Lizzie split when she heard that. I can't say as I blamed her. What daughter could handle that so soon after her mother died? Of all Shirley's faults—and believe me, she has plenty—hurting Lizzie like that was the worst.

"But it was enough to finally get me off my butt. Sold the house and rented the place in Royal Palm Breeze sight unseen off Craigslist. I figured a change of scenery would be good for me, help me move on. And get Shirley off my back once and for all."

Jack's laugh was hollow. "I guess I shouldn't have been surprised when Shirley showed up at Royal Palm Breeze the day after my moving truck left. I gave her an honest-to-god ultimatum as soon as she got there, though."

This was all news to Vince.

Jack looked at him. "I probably pushed her right into your dad's arms. I'm sorry."

Vince shrugged. "Don't be. If it weren't for Shirley, I'd still be stuck there with Tony myself.

"But for both our sakes, let's just hope neither of them can find us here."

# CHAPTER FIVE

VINCE WOKE TO a soft slapping sound outside. For a while he lay in bed, trying to figure out where he was and how he'd gotten there. Gradually, pieces of the last day and a half came together in his mind as he re-traced the journey from Royal Palm Breeze to Moon Beach and the lemon yellow cottage in Whispering Pines.

A shower and a cup of coffee cleared his head. It was time to look around, go for a run. A wooden walkway leading through the woods beckoned. The walkway had been neglected for years and was overgrown with weeds. Vince followed it to its end and was amazed to find himself alone on a sandy beach. His memories of the Jersey shore from a distant childhood were of crowds, transistor radios tuned to the ball game, and the heavy smell of fried clams, chili dogs, and Coppertone.

In the last several years, even after moving to Royal Palm Breeze, Vince hadn't been to the beach. Tony kept him too busy planting and tending heirloom tomatoes in the back yard. At first, Vince didn't mind since his mother seemed to enjoy them. But after she died they had far more plants than they could ever use. By late summer the stench of tomatoes rotting on the black plastic mulch sickened Vince whenever he went into the yard to weed. Vince exhaled sharply to get that memory out of his head.

When he inhaled again, he breathed in salt air and flowers. Vince kicked off his shoes and dug his toes into the soft sand. He sat and let sand sift through his fingers. For the first time in years, he heard waves hit the beach, retreat, and hit again. He had forgotten what it was like to sit, just sit, and he realized how good the sun felt, warming his skin, warming something inside him as well. In a few minutes he would put his shoes back on to run along the beach, to run as far as he could into the distance.

"Lovely, yes?" Vince opened his eyes and squinted into the sun before focusing on the figure in front of him. Her gnarled hands rested on a walking stick covered with psychedelic painted swirls. She wore a neon pink Red Sox cap and a Nine Inch Nails T-shirt.

"Welcome to Moon Beach. I'm Ernestine. You must be Vince. You're over at Bernie's and Anne's now, aren't you?" He was startled that the tiny hand with blue veins grasped his so firmly in a solid handshake.

She lowered herself to a heavy log on the beach and looked slowly up and down at his six foot frame, well-toned from daily running. "Well, they can sure use some help, and I suspect you can, too. Glad you found each other." Word seemed to travel quickly in Moon Beach.

"You live around here?" Vince finally asked.

Ernestine nodded. She pointed toward a strand of cottages far down the shoreline. "Been in Moon Beach just about my whole adult life. Got married here, and when my ex decided to move inland, I had to choose between him and the water."

She looked out at the beach and smiled. "Best decision I ever made to stand up to him and say, 'I'm staying here.' My heart and soul will always be in Moon Beach.

"Lots of places along the coast have changed so's you can't recognize them anymore, but Moon Beach works to keep itself behind the times. I don't know how long we can stay this way. We're trying, though."

Ernestine looked directly at Vince. Her eyes were pale blue and rimmed with a deep turquoise, as if she'd soaked the color up directly from the sea.

Vince knew that Ernestine was waiting for him to say something. He felt he could take all day to say it and she'd be right there waiting for him.

"I've just stood up for myself, too." Vince was surprised that the words had come out of his mouth. "I hope it's going to work out okay." He realized he felt lighter after saying it, that the dull heaviness he'd been carrying was beginning to lift.

Ernestine continued to look directly at Vince. Then she picked something up from the beach and pressed it into Vince's hand.

"Here," she said. "Moon Beach has its own magic. You'll see. Hold on to this." She stood up and headed down the beach toward the strand of cottages.

Vince looked down. He held a piece of shell, white and purple, worn by the sea into an almost perfect circle.

What did she mean, its own magic?

# CHAPTER SIX

SHIRLEY DRIFTED FROM sleep into semi-consciousness and looked up at Tony, confused. She must have been dreaming, imagining one of Vince's ricotta pies. How could that possibly make Tony feel bad?

"I don't feel so good," Tony repeated. "I mebbe having a heart attack." This time Shirley heard him, and she opened her eyes. He was gray. He looked like her father had when he was dying. She snapped awake.

"I'm gonna call 911 for an ambulance," she said and reached for the phone.

"No. We drive." Tony closed his eyes and groaned. Shirley scrambled into jeans and a shirt. Would she have time to put on some make-up, fix her hair?

Tony groaned again. Probably not.

Tony crawled into the rumpled clothes he'd thrown on the floor before going to bed. "Let's go. Hurry."

Shirley had never driven Tony's big SUV before, and she savored the feeling of the steering wheel, the way the vehicle responded to her touch.

"Faster. *Fretta.*" For someone in the middle of a heart

attack, Tony was awfully bossy, Shirley thought, but it was fun to lower her foot some more on the gas pedal. At 4 A.M. the roads were empty and she stepped harder on the gas. The SUV sailed along the road and she concentrated on driving while Tony moaned in the passenger seat. Good thing the hospital was on the way to the mall so she already knew how to get there.

She squealed to a stop in front of the Emergency Room entrance. An orderly came out with a wheelchair and Shirley parked as the man wheeled Tony into the hospital.

When she got inside, the receptionist pointed through a set of double doors. Shirley walked right past the waiting room filled with people in various states of pain. Years ago, when she'd cut her hand and gone to an emergency room for stitches, she'd waited for hours to see a doctor, and here was Tony sailing right to the front of the line. Figures.

Tony was already hooked to a monitor when Shirley got to his bedside. The nurse looked at her. "We're trying to make your husband comfortable right now. Once we confirm that his vital signs are stable, we'll take him upstairs for a CAT scan." Shirley nodded, but she didn't have a clue what any of it meant.

A couple of minutes later, an orderly in blue scrubs came in and started to wheel Tony's bed out of the room. The nurse looked at Shirley. "You can sit in the waiting room. We'll call you when Mr. O'Brien is back." Shirley barely heard the woman but she nodded and headed back out the double doors.

She was still not fully awake, and hungry after eating so little of last night's dinner. Would she have time to find the hospital cafeteria, or better yet, drive out to the Dixie

Grill for a real breakfast? Then she remembered she didn't have any money and she was stuck there in the hospital with a bunch of sick people, just waiting to breathe in their germs.

Four people dozed in the waiting room. An infomercial for an at-home business that guaranteed an annual income of six figures working ten hours a week blared out of the TV bolted high on the wall. It sounded like a good deal to Shirley and she wrote down the phone number. Depending on Tony for money was the pits. Depending on any man for money was the pits, but it was all she knew.

"Mrs. O'Brien?" The woman came right up to Shirley's face so she must have been talking to her. "Your husband is finished with the CAT scan so you can go in and see him now." Shirley nodded and followed her. What was this O'Brien crap?

Tony looked pretty rested for someone who was making everyone jump up and down in the middle of the night. "Tony, what's with this O'Brien crap?" Shirley asked as soon as they were alone in the room.

"The Irish side of the family was all priests. Might as well suck up to them if you're gonna die."

Shirley didn't believe him, but she dropped it. There was plenty about Tony that she didn't know. She was hungry, tired and she just wanted to go back to Tony's and take a shower.

"You're looking pretty good so far, Mr. O'Brien. But I think we're going to admit you for observation just in case." Shirley hated that everyone in the hospital wore scrubs so you couldn't tell the doctors from the cleaning crew. This one had a clipboard and a stethoscope, so

Shirley guessed she wasn't there to mop the floor.

She looked at Shirley and smiled. "You look exhausted. Why don't you go home and rest for a while and come back around lunchtime? By then we should have a clearer idea of what's going on with your husband."

Shirley was thrilled by those words. But the next were even better: "Why don't you take his valuables with you for safekeeping?" Shirley grabbed the plastic bag with Tony's wallet and almost ran out of the room without another word.

Tony grunted and she remembered he was there.

"How are you feeling?" It was the first time she asked.

"You going to the house?" Tony looked worried.

"Yeah, I thought I'd freshen up a bit, maybe bring you back some clothes, your toothbrush." Shirley smiled at him. He grimaced.

The woman with the stethoscope came back into the room and Shirley practically flew to the parking lot.

She was free.

# CHAPTER SEVEN

ONCE IN THE car, Shirley tore through Tony's wallet. Out of state driver's license for John Anthony O'Brien. Absolutely no credit cards. A single twenty dollar bill. Shirley almost swooned at the prospect of spending it on sweet potato pancakes at the Dixie Grill.

Then she thought about having some time to snoop through Tony's things at home. She pulled through the drive-through window at McDonald's instead.

Back at the house, Shirley showered and began going through Tony's bureau. Other than some tiny black silk briefs, she found nothing unusual. She worked her way methodically through the house: everything in the closets, suitcases, boxes in the garage. Nothing. Not even bills. It was as if Tony, or whoever he was, didn't actually exist.

The kitchen was last, since Shirley had never seen Tony in the kitchen and it was hardly her favorite room. Still, he had to have money, credit cards, something, somewhere. She already knew the freezer was empty. That left the pantry, filled mostly with Vince's baking supplies: glass canisters of flour, sugar, nuts, a tin of dog biscuits.

Dog biscuits? Tony hated dogs.

Shirley grabbed the red Milk-Bones tin and yanked off the lid. The tin appeared to be full of dog biscuits, but Shirley was beginning to figure out that things with Tony were not always what they appeared to be. She dumped the container into the sink. Drivers' licenses. Passports. Credit cards. Different names, but Tony's mug on them. She looked closely. There were even IDs for her!

She sat for a long time, staring at her picture on an Oklahoma driver's license for someone named Shirley Beaver, trying to figure out what, exactly, was going on. She'd never even been to Oklahoma.

The telephone ring knocked her back to reality.

"Shirley, where the hell are you?" Tony sounded pretty robust for someone dying from a heart attack. "Bring me something to eat. This hospital serves dog crap."

Shirley looked in the refrigerator. The barbecue, now that the grease floated in white islands on top of gray liquid, looked alarming. She slapped some cheese and lettuce on a leftover bun instead and threw it in a plastic bag.

She didn't know what to do with her find, so she tossed everything into the dog biscuit tin and stuck it back in the pantry. She would confront Tony and find out just who and what he was as soon as she got to the hospital.

A woman in blue scrubs was typing on a hospital laptop when Shirley walked into Tony's room.

Shirley wanted to ask about the bogus IDs. Instead, she managed a weak smile and said, "How are you feeling?" She tried to sound like she cared. She tossed the sandwich on Tony's bed.

"Mr. O'Brien seems to be doing pretty well." The

woman stopped typing to look up at Shirley and speak. According to her name tag she was Jodie Sanders, R.N.

"We're going to do some more tests. Then we'll keep him overnight just to make sure he's stable. He's lucky he'll have you to take care of him after that." She flashed a big smile at both of them. Jodie Sanders, R.N., didn't know squat about Shirley.

Shirley and Tony glowered at each other. Neither of them felt lucky at this point. Tony chewed his sandwich and swallowed the dry bread without comment. Nurse Sanders' rubber soles squeaked on the linoleum as she left the room.

"Tony, what the hell's going on? What's with the phony IDs in the pantry? Who the hell are you?" If there was a chance Tony was going to keel over and die, Shirley wanted to get the straight scoop before he did.

Tony looked at Shirley and his eyes widened. He gasped and grabbed his chest. Shirley waited for him to answer the question. She hated these theatrical gestures.

"Tony?"

Tony's monitor started to emit a loud, insistent tone. Shirley could hear Nurse Sanders' rubber soles racing back down the hall. Within seconds, the room filled with hospital staff and Shirley was escorted out of the room.

By the time Jodie Sanders, R.N., got back to Shirley, Tony had been wheeled out of his room and rushed into the ICU.

So much for his speedy recovery.

# CHAPTER EIGHT

BERNIE MOTIONED VINCE to join Jack and him on Bernie's big deck when he saw Vince step off the walkway after his run.

"Ah, I see you've already discovered the beach. Moon Beach is a good place to invent, reinvent, yourself. We're all doing it here to some extent." Bernie fished an olive out of his glass and chewed it. "High blood pressure," he said. "The only way I can stand the pills is if they're tucked inside a pimento.

"I've got a couple of clients here and some in the state capital, though my days of working twenty-four seven are over, thank heaven. Anne won't let me work like that any more. She's busy at her bookstore most days, and you can see it's pretty laid back out here. I go to the capital once or twice a month, but I'm a lot happier with the pace here at Whispering Pines." He leaned back in the deck chair and stretched out.

"Anyway, you can probably tell that some of the cottages need work." Bernie chuckled. "I sure didn't learn anything practical in law school. There's a workshop full of tools. Most of them still in the original packing, just begging to get out and do something. I thought I'd use them once we moved here, but it hasn't happened yet.

"If you're willing to help with some painting, maintenance, you're welcome to stay as long as you want. We're never full even during the height of the season. Lately we've just had a couple of overnighters, maybe two or three days at the most. Good thing we don't depend on this for our living. I guess this is our hobby, but Anne might have some other ideas for the cottages."

Each cottage was painted a different color, although the paint was faded and peeling. The little signs in front of each cottage reflected the color: Lemonade, Limeade, Flamingo, Blue Moon.

"I'm game," Jack said. "It'll be good to get my mind on something constructive. Not to mention my body. And reinventing myself sounds like a great idea about now."

Vince nodded. "Me too. Sounds wonderful. I'm pretty good with my hands and I'm used to keeping busy."

"Start anywhere." Bernie waved his hand out toward the little cottages. "Whatever you end up with is bound to be better than what you started with." He realized that while he was referring to the faded cottages, the description fit just about everyone's situation in Moon Beach as well.

That was the thing about Moon Beach.

Vince and Jack sorted through the maze of tools in the workshop. Bernie was right; most of the power tools had never been used. Jack held up a mop and an electric power washer to Vince. "Choose your weapon," he said.

Vince grabbed the mop. "I'm an old-fashioned kind of guy. Let's go." He picked up a bucket and a gallon jug of heavy duty cleaner. "I'll start with the kitchens and bath. I can do the indoors if you focus on the outside. Then we can switch if we get bored."

For the next couple of weeks, Jack and Vince threw themselves into work. First they cleaned, inside and out, getting rid of old cobwebs, peeling paint, and general dirt and grime. There was a visible difference just with soap, water, and heavy scrubbing.

Then they started serious work on Blue Moon and Flamingo, replacing punky boards and spackling nicks in the plaster before transforming the faded buildings with fresh paint. Their muscles began to reflect the physical effort they put in each day.

Painting the moldings was what finally did it for Vince. Cleaning, priming, even painting the walls: all that was a start. But by painting the crisp white lines to frame the windows and doors, he saw a transformation so concrete and so magic that anything felt possible to him.

If hard work could make such a difference with the cottages, who knew what else it could change?

Vince closed his can of paint and headed for the workshop sink to clean the brushes at the end of a work day. Now both the Blue Moon and Flamingo cottages looked worthy of their names.

"I'm beat." Jack came into the workshop with a roller tray and a paint can. His dark hair, already streaked with gray, was dotted with bright pink paint. When he rubbed his eye he added another streak across his face. "How about you?"

"You know, ever since we've been working on the cottages, I've hardly had a chance to talk to Bernie and

Anne," Vince said. "I mean, they've been terrific to let me stay here like I was an old friend when they didn't know me from Adam. Do you think they'd mind if we took a day off to fix them a big dinner?"

"Are you kidding me? Once they find out about your cooking they're gonna want to see you with a wooden spoon, not a paintbrush, in your hand. Sounds great."

The back of the Jeep was piled high with grocery bags when Vince headed back from food shopping the next morning. It was his first time exploring the town of Moon Beach, with its quaint main street lined with palm trees and brightly painted shops. Two small shopping centers provided the more mundane necessities like groceries and hardware for residents who weren't looking for souvenirs or T-shirts. Vince had visited them before to buy  food and supplies for fixing up the cottages. This morning he'd gone to three different stores to get everything he needed for dinner, but it felt like an adventure and not a chore.

Still, he spent as much time looking in the rear view mirror as looking at the road ahead. Just in case.

"My taste buds are revving up already," Jack said as he helped Vince unload the bags. "Just tell me what I can do to help." Vince put Jack to work first with the big knife, chopping vegetables so piles of red, green, purple, and white stood ready, waiting to be incorporated into sauces at just the right moment.

By early afternoon, Vince was covered with a white haze of flour from rolling pasta and making pastries. Red sauces bubbled on the stove, cheese and egg mixtures sat on the counter, and pans were carefully lined up for the final assembly process. Vince was precise and methodical. Tony had wanted his dinner served at exactly 6 P.M., not a minute before or after, and this taught Vince to time his preparations carefully.

Jack surveyed the room, which had taken on the careful organization of an operating room under Vince's direction. "Vince, all I can do is stand back and marvel. And then do whatever you tell me to do to pull off this event."

Vince grinned at his friend. "Don't worry. I've got everything under control." And suddenly he realized that he did have control, at least of this day. He felt terrific.

"Oh, good Lord. That was the best meal I've had in years." Anne reached for another slice of ricotta pie. "I had no idea you could cook like this, Vince." She looked at him. "Really, a restaurant could make a killing with food like this. I've never had eggplant so light and crisp. And the lasagna! But it's your desserts that really slay me." She dipped her fork into Bernie's tiramisu and closed her eyes as she slid the fork into her mouth. "Umm..." Tendrils of dark hair flecked with gray spilled across her face as she leaned back.

"Anne's right," Bernie said. "This was sensational. I can't think of another meal that even comes close." He reached over and gently pushed the wayward hair back behind Anne's ear before stroking her cheek. Then he scraped off the last bit of ricotta pie from her plate and groaned contentedly.

Vince wasn't accustomed to hearing any praise for his cooking. He felt light-headed, and it wasn't from the wine. "I'm glad you enjoyed it. You two have helped me more than you could possibly know by letting me stay here. I'd love to be able to pay you back somehow."

Anne took another bite of tiramisu and said, "We've been talking about ways to get more people interested in the bookstore. We'd like to expand it to get more folks to come in. Add coffee, cold drinks, some desserts. Seems like sometimes people want to eat more than they want to read."

She looked directly at Vince. "Your pastries would be the perfect touch. You think you might be interested in doing some baking for us? We just need to figure out our financials before going too far out on a limb with the café idea."

"You want me to look at the numbers for you?" Jack spoke up. "Remember, I'm an accountant. I'd love to help if I can."

Anne looked from Jack to Vince. "Absolutely! Between the ledgers and the tiramisu, the two of you might be the answer to my prayers right now."

Vince couldn't believe his good luck. Talk about the answer to a prayer.

It sounded too good to be true.

# CHAPTER NINE

ANNE WRESTLED WITH the lock for a minute before the lime green door swung open. *Words & More* was painted in bright letters on the big glass window. Colorful book jackets set amid beach toys and seashells beckoned from the sidewalk. A lime green bench in front of the store invited people to sit outside before or after a visit inside the shop.

"What do you think?" Anne looked at Vince. "We're a full-service book store. We'll order anything for anyone, but we're mostly a beach read kind of place. Mysteries, romance, best sellers, vampires, and a big kids' section. Plus we sell used books and showcase local authors."

Vince looked around. He hadn't had much shopping experience except Walmart and wherever else Tony wanted to go, but he liked the feel of the shop right away. It fit in with the rest of Moon Beach's little downtown, colorful and welcoming. The space was cozy, with enough room for several wicker chairs with bright cushions. A folding screen hid a second room, empty except for a long library table and some small round tables.

"I like it." An image of his mother in her rocking chair reading *Winnie the Pooh* to him when he was a child flashed into his mind. "It feels homey and comfortable."

"I think if we had a little café here with sweets– especially your sweets, Vince–we'd get more people to come in, look around, decide to stay awhile. There's no place in town, really, for folks to just drop in and chat. I'd love to see us become that place, a real community center. What do you think?"

Vince was already rearranging the space to fit a small display case and deciding what desserts he would put in it. He envisioned plates of pastries on the library table, maybe an espresso maker at the end.

"Vince?" Anne waved her hands in front of his face and he snapped back to the present. "Are you interested?"

Was he interested?

Was she kidding?

Vince laughed. "Y'know, I've already arranged the café space for you. The refrigerated display case can go there." He pointed to one side of the room. "Then the espresso maker can fit on a table next to it. When can I start?"

"I think you already have." Anne grinned at him. "We haven't really used this space very well, basically just for storage. But with something to eat here it would be different. Your tiramisu ought to draw in some new customers, I hope."

Vince looked out the window. "Vagrants as well?" He pointed to a gray-haired figure sitting on the bench outside, smoking a cigarillo.

Anne looked up. "Vagrants? Oh, good Lord, she'll love that. She probably has her finger in more prime real estate than Donald Trump. C'mon, I want you to meet my bookstore partner."

Vince followed Anne outside.

"Vince, I'd like you to meet Ernestine."

The woman stood up and looked directly at Vince with those unforgettable bright eyes. She gripped his hand into a firm shake.

"Oh, we are already friends. I'm so glad to see you again, young man." She took another puff on her cigarillo.

# CHAPTER TEN

VINCE WAS ON edge. After several years that dragged slowly and painfully to the beat of Tony's demands, he now found life moving dangerously fast. What was he doing, thinking he could draw customers into Words & More with his pastries? What if people decided they didn't like his desserts? Even worse, what if he couldn't follow through enough to deliver?

Anne was counting on him. He was counting on himself. What if he failed Anne and Ernestine? What if he failed himself?

Jack seemed on edge, too. He'd spent days poring over the financial statements for Words & More and hoped that the advice he'd offered would point them in the right direction. It was a tough call in this economy for any small business to stay afloat, and taking on the added expense of serving food, even Vince's pastries, was a gamble.

Tension filled the lemon yellow cottage. Enough that Jack and Vince had barely spoken to each other that morning. Jack finally left the cottage and went out to the workshop.

Vince's hands were immersed in soapy dishwater when he heard the crunch of tires on the gravel driveway. Wary, he watched as an unfamiliar car stopped and the driver's door swung open.

Sinewy female legs unfolded from the driver's seat. She stood up, stretched, and shook loose a mane of long red hair. When she turned to face the cottage, glints of sunlight danced through her hair. Vince caught his breath and held it.

She headed toward the yellow cottage and trotted up the stairs to the deck. Vince stood, immobilized, hands still in the dishwater.

She knocked and he walked toward the door, wiping his hands on his shirt as he did.

She knocked again, louder this time.

"Daddy?"

Vince heard footsteps running up the stairs. He watched as Jack grabbed the young woman in a bear hug. "Lizzie! You made it!"

"Daddy!" The two of them drew apart to look at each other, then embraced again, both laughing as they did so. Vince stepped out onto the deck to join them.

"Vince, this is my daughter, Lizzie." Jack looked from Lizzie to Vince. "Vince is, well, I guess you could call him my lifeboat partner."

Tears were streaming down both Jack and Lizzie's faces. Vince could see the resemblance between the two, the high cheekbones and clear green eyes. Lizzie was in her mid-twenties, Vince guessed, and Jack could almost pass for her older brother now that the lines of strain had vanished from his face. Jack looked ten years younger than he had earlier that morning.

Vince felt a sharp ache of longing as he watched them. What would a reunion between his father and him look like? Was it even possible? Could Tony ever be happy to see his only son?

"Come on, Bernie'll be thrilled to see you finally got here." Jack led her down the cottage steps and over to the house with the big wraparound deck.

Later that day Lizzie, Jack, Anne, and Vince sat comfortably on the deck and watched Bernie flip tuna steaks on the grill. During dinner, Jack spoke and laughed more than he had in all the time since Vince first met him.

Anne poured more wine for all of them. "Lizzie, how long can you stay?"

Lizzie's face darkened for the first time all day. "I don't know. I'm sort of between things right now."

Anne caught the look. "Well, we have plenty of room and you're more than welcome for as long as you want, dear."

"Yes, especially if you don't mind getting your hands dirty and helping us spruce the place up a bit," Bernie added.

"I'd like that. I can clean. And I can paint." Lizzie spoke very softly.

"The studio cottage will be just right for you. It's small, but perfect for one person." Anne smiled.

Whispering Pines was filling up just the way she hoped it would.

# CHAPTER ELEVEN

THE DAY AFTER Shirley brought Tony home from the hospital she said, "We're gonna go find them."

Tony thought she was nuts, but he was a desperate man who wanted nothing more than a big plate of Vince's eggplant rollatini. He was ready to try almost anything to get Vince back.

"Shirley, we don't know nothing about where they went. Or if they're even together."

She cocked her head sideways. "I might have an idea."

For the first time in weeks, Tony was interested in what she had to say. "Yeah?"

"Well, Jack talked about these friends of his somewhere farther south he wanted to visit. I think they kept in touch."

"So you want us to drive 'somewhere farther south' in hopes we can run into them somewhere? Don't sound like much of a plan to me." Shirley could be so lame.

She shook her shoulders and her breasts swayed back and forth ever so slightly. "How's about I give you the street address? Will that be 'somewhere farther south' enough for you?"

"Yeah?"

She pulled an envelope out of her purse and waved it in front of Tony. He grabbed it. Sure enough, it was addressed to Jack. The letter had gone first to Jack's old address and been forwarded to Royal Palm Breeze. More importantly, it had a return address label stuck on the front.

"I looked in the mailbox every couple of days to see if there were any checks or anything for me. Bills and stuff like that I just threw away. But this came addressed to Jack so I opened it." She held up a birthday card and read the message: "Thinking of you, Jack. Anne and I would love to see you. Come visit! Bernie."

Tony wasn't convinced. "I dunno. Jack never even got the card."

"But this Bernie guy sent it. That means they were friends," Shirley said. "And I remember Jack talking about wanting to visit him."

"What makes you think Vince went with him?" Tony still wasn't convinced.

"Where else would he go? What are the chances he'd head back to Jersey?"

Tony knew the chances of Vince heading back north were slim to non-existent. Shirley acted like she was a freaking rocket scientist sometimes.

"So what do you suggest instead, Einstein?" She cocked her head again. Tony scowled at her. How could they possibly spend days, maybe weeks, traveling together without killing each other?

Tony thought with desperation about Vince's fresh pasta, the little rum cakes. Even hospital food was better than Shirley's cooking.

What did he have to lose? At least he'd be eating out while they were on the road.

"Okay, we'll go. But you better be right about this." He sifted through a stack of credit cards and fake IDs before picking several of each to cover their expenses.

Tony watched as Shirley lugged her huge suitcase out to the SUV. He thought how happy he'd been the last time he saw her dragging that same suitcase, but into his house. How times changed.

Maybe they would find Jack and Vince at this guy Bernie's house. And Shirley'd lug that big suitcase back over to Jack. Then Vince would come back where he belonged, doing what Tony thought he should be doing: taking care of Tony.

The prospect made his heart race with anticipation.

"Come on, let's get moving." Tony entered Bernie's address into the GPS while Shirley wrestled her suitcase into the back of the car. His heart was still racing ten miles down the road. He hoped it was just the excitement of getting away from what had become a prison for him and not another heart attack.

Shirley was bouncing up and down in the passenger seat to some god-awful pop music station. Her breasts were keeping rhythm with the band so Tony tuned out the sound and tried to keep his eyes on the road.

Tony saw a billboard for an Olive Garden when they were about two-thirds of the way to Moon Beach. He slowed down for the exit. This would be as good a place as any to stop for the night. The interstate was crammed with motels and they'd just find one near the restaurant.

"Oh, Mexican!" Shirley squealed when she saw the neon La Cantina restaurant sign as they came off the highway exit onto the service road.

"Italian." Tony barely opened his lips when he said it. He pulled into a Hampton Inn and parked near the lobby.

As soon as they checked in, they got back in the car and Tony drove directly to the Olive Garden. Shirley started to pout but gave up since Tony was already inside the restaurant. He was seated at a booth and looking at the menu when she got to the door.

Shirley ordered a Margarita before she got to the table and slurped most of it down as soon as it arrived. She closed her eyes, savoring the warm tingling growing in the back of her head.

"Ma'am?" The waiter stood above her with an order pad. Shirley set down her Margarita and looked at the waiter.

"Do you have any Mexican dishes?"

"We're an Italian restaurant, ma'am."

"Shirley, just pick some damn thing or I'll pick it for you. I'm too hungry to waste time pretending we're in Acapulco."

Shirley frowned at Tony and pointed to something on the menu. "I'll have that."

"Excellent choice, ma'am. And for you, sir?"

Tony ordered enough to feed a soccer team. He hadn't had real food in what felt like months. Not that this was real food, but it was closer than anything he'd seen since the last of Vince's casseroles was gone.

Shirley was buzzed on her second Margarita by the time her pasta arrived. She ordered a third. Neither of them spoke as Tony shoveled spoonful after spoonful of food into his grateful mouth.

It was the most satisfying experience either of them had had since shortly after Shirley moved into Tony's, but they couldn't bear to admit it to each other or to themselves. They passed the evening in olive oil and tequila oblivion, and neither was unhappy for the moment.

# CHAPTER TWELVE

THE TWO-LANE road followed the coast for several miles. At some points they could see water in the distance. Little side roads with tiny cottages and mobile homes led down to the beach. As far as Shirley was concerned, this was backwoods, backwater country. The whole area gave her the creeps.

"Slow down. I think we're there." Shirley looked from the envelope in her hand to the weathered and peeling sign for Whispering Pines Cottages to her right. "At least it's the same number."

"You have reached your destination." The voice on the GPS offered its confirmation.

"This place looks run-down as all crap. You sure this is it?"

"I think so." She wasn't at all sure. She'd been expecting a house in a civilized neighborhood instead of a dirt driveway that snaked through the woods to god knows where.

What if neither of them was there? Even worse, she suddenly realized, what if they were there? If Vince was willing to go back with Tony, where would that leave her? She wished she'd thought through all the possibilities before giving Tony the address.

She wanted to turn around right then and drive straight through back to Royal Palm Breeze. Why give Vince the opportunity to go back with Tony and cut her out of the picture? She knew Jack didn't want her around. Nobody wanted her around. For an instant the awful reality paralyzed her.

The crunch of the SUV's tires on the gravel driveway brought her back to the moment. She'd just have to face life head on. She knew how to survive and she'd figure something out. She always did.

She shook her head so the curls fell around her face in what she hoped was an appealing look and got out of the car.

"That looks like Jack's Jeep." Shirley trotted over to the Jeep and peered in the windows. Loud Hawaiian print covered the seats and wraparound shades hung from the rear-view mirror.

"Shirley, you know how many cars like that there are in beach towns? It's not Jack's. Look at those seat covers. It's some kid's car. And those plates. They're local."

A door opened onto the deck above them. "Oh, that must be Bernie coming out now," Shirley said. "Let me talk to him. You know my way of charming people. I ought to be able to draw him out so's he'll tell us if he's seen them."

Tony said nothing.

She attached a smile to her face and yelled "Yoo-hoo y'all!" in what she thought was a Southern accent.

Bernie's years as a lawyer had helped him develop a

well-honed bullshit detection system that was now registering maximum overload. He sensed it was definitely not the time to answer any probing questions these folks might ask, starting with the time of day and date.

The woman waved an envelope in his face and started talking: loud, shrill and fast. It was a bad combination.

Just then Bernie heard a commotion and turned to see what was causing the racket coming from the lemon yellow cottage.

He broke into a broad grin. He didn't know what was going to happen next, but he was pretty sure he was going to enjoy it.

# CHAPTER THIRTEEN

"HOLY SHIT! I think it's them." Vince was sitting on the deck reading a new cookbook when he saw the big black SUV pull into the clearing. He dove to the floor and crawled into the cottage on his hands and knees, hoping against hope that he hadn't been seen. Jack came racing out of the kitchen and they both peered out the living room windows from behind the blinds.

"Can't be." The tan drained out of Vince's face when brassy curls that could only be Shirley's emerged from the vehicle. "Shit."

Jack looked at him. "Is that all you can say? We've got to do something!"

"Do something? Then come up with an idea, bird brain! We don't have all day."

Bird brain.

"That's it! Come on." Jack disappeared into his bedroom and came back with a large cardboard box. He opened it and threw a pile of yellow and white feathers at Vince. "Put this on. I'll give you the head in a minute."

"What the hell is this?"

Vince couldn't believe it. His dad had come to try to take him back to his old life and Jack picked that instant to go completely batshit insane. Talk about timing.

"Come on, just put the chicken suit on. At least they won't recognize us when we drive out of here."

Vince stared at him in disbelief.

"You got a better idea? Here, your feet go in this way."

They scrambled into the suits and slid the heads on. They were surprisingly realistic looking. For gigantic chickens.

Shirley had headed over to talk with Bernie after she'd given the Jeep the once over. Jack gave a silent prayer of thanks that he'd changed the license plates as soon as they arrived in Moon Beach. And that Lizzie had given him the seat covers to celebrate his new lease on life.

Jack turned to Vince. "Hurry up before she has a chance to wag those things at Bernie and make him stupid. Come on."

Their webbed feet made a racket on the wooden steps. Three heads turned in their direction. Tony, Shirley, and Bernie watched wordlessly as two giant chickens got into the Jeep.

Jack had to slip his hands out of the wings to drive. He hoped they wouldn't notice. The chicken head was not made for driving and his peripheral vision was crap.

"Wave to Bernie like this is business as usual when we go by," Jack instructed Vince. "They might not notice I have hands."

Tony and Shirley stood with their mouths wide open as the Jeep drove past and the chicken in the passenger seat waved to them. Bernie waved back and succeeded in keeping from laughing out loud.

The Jeep continued down the long curved drive and out of sight.

Bernie wondered which of his visitors would speak first. He waited.

"What the fuck was that?" Shirley and Tony said in unison.

"The tenants in the yellow cottage. Now, is there something I can help you with?" Bernie smiled serenely at the two of them and thought they'd both look a lot better with their mouths closed.

No, he'd never heard of this Bernie person. Nor Jack. Nor Vince. Yes, he'd lived here for years. They must have the wrong address. Perhaps the wrong state?

"Currently I have a family of pigeons living in the green cottage," Bernie said. This was unfortunately the truth. "But they might be heading farther south for the winter migration. If so, and if you are interested in a winter rental, I might be able to accommodate you. Would you care to leave your names?"

Tony was shaking with anger. He'd been hoping for hand-rolled cannelloni and he got six foot tall chickens instead. Chickens that drove cars.

"Great idea, Shirley. I'm getting out of here before some frigging monster pigeons show up." He got in the car and slammed the door.

Shirley turned to speak to Bernie but he'd already begun walking back up the stairs to the deck. He just hoped he could make it inside before he burst into laughter.

# CHAPTER FOURTEEN

"WHERE TO? I can't see so hot through the feathers."

"Go to Big Al's. It's not the kind of place either Shirley or Tony would go. We can park behind the wall so they won't even see the Jeep."

Big Al's was also less than a quarter mile away, which was about all Jack felt comfortable driving. He wondered what kind of motor vehicle violations he would rack up if he got stopped by the police on the way there, or if they'd have to invent new ones especially for him.

Jack pulled into Big Al's side lot without incident. Big Al's, which claimed to serve the best breakfasts in the world, looked like a derelict rat trap from the street. It was intentional, Al said, to keep people from away from even thinking of stopping in.

Besides, he'd much rather be tending an omelet or cutting biscuits than scraping peeling paint. His customers, locals mostly, liked it just fine the way it was.

"We should keep our heads on till we get inside just in case. It'll be fun to see Al's reaction. Let's go." They walked up the steps, careful of the uneven planks and exposed nail heads, and walked in the door.

Big Al bragged to his friends that nothing could surprise him. Still, he hesitated a fraction of a second before he was able to speak.

"Welcome, um, ladies. Would you prefer a booth or the counter?"

Vince had already headed for a booth and Jack followed. The teenage waitress pleaded with Al with wild eyes and Al motioned her back behind the counter. The first chicken's head started spinning until it came off and Jack emerged from within. Vince followed and Al looked slowly from one to the other as he pulled up a chair at the end of the booth.

"Boys, I assume there's a story here." He turned to face the young waitress. "Brittany, can you bring these fellas some ice water? Must be hotter'n blazes in them things. Don't worry, they won't bite. Or cluck. Or whatever oversized chickens do."

Al turned back to the table. "Well?"

"Let's get Bernie over here first." Jack picked up his cell phone to call.

Jack started right in as soon as Bernie walked in. "We might not have been, uh, as clear as possible when we arrived in town about just what we were leaving behind and why. And how." By the time he described leaving Royal Palm Breeze, Bernie and Al were both shaking their heads in disbelief.

"Glory halleluh." Al wiped his face with a bandana. "You Yankees sure take the cake. We got ways of disappearing folks down here, you know what I'm saying? But giant chicken suits?" He burst into laughter.

Vince sounded worried. "I just want to know why you

had those chicken costumes, Jack. That might be even scarier than Shirley and Tony showing up."

"Remember Jason, that ditzy temp Anne had helping with inventory when I was looking over the accounting? He came around one day asking if anyone wanted to order takeout from Geppetto's for lunch," Jack said. "I'd brought lunch, but I thought I'd bring something home for supper. I told him what I wanted and forgot all about it until I was leaving for the day. I asked Jason if he'd forgotten and he said no, it was on order and should arrive in a week or so. I thought it was just one of his dumb-ass remarks.

"So a couple of days later this big box arrived at the shop filled with chicken costumes and for the longest time I couldn't figure it out how or why I got it. And then I remembered Jason."

"So?" Vince looked at him. "I still don't get it."

"I'd asked for chicken costaletta. All I can figure is he mucked that up into chicken costumes. Must have spent the whole afternoon researching that instead of counting books. I brought the box home to ask Anne what to do since the bookstore must have gotten billed for them. Then I forgot all about them until the second I saw Shirley get out of the car."

"Don't you dare think about returning those chicken suits, my friend." Bernie wagged his finger at Jack. "I've never laughed so hard in my life. I'll pick up the tab for them.

"You never know when a giant chicken costume might come in handy."

# CHAPTER FIFTEEN

"WHICH ONE DO you like best?" Anne held up a fan of paint chips. "I want it to feel cozy and inviting. Restful. Different somehow. Like a cocoon."

"That ugly purple isn't going to do it."

"The tag calls it Pale Aubergine, Ernestine. Think of it as a young eggplant waiting to become one of Vince's creations."

"Well, all I see is a giant bruise. Pick something else." Ernestine was insistent.

Lizzie held up a soft brown. "How about this? It won't clash with the bright colors in the main room. I don't know; it's sort of a nice mocha. Maybe make people want a cup of coffee?"

"They're more likely to want sweet tea. But you're right. It's a good contrast to the other room. And it's a perfect backdrop for having a drop dead fantastic dessert! What do you think, Vince?" Anne turned to him.

Vince had no idea what to think. His head was swimming and the last thing he could concentrate on was paint chips. Here he was, in a room with three generations of women who were treating him like a human being, who cared about his opinion. Three women, each strong and vibrant, and all distinctively beautiful.

How could he think about paint colors?

"I like it," Ernestine said. So it was settled. Mocha Sundae it would be.

Mocha Sundae turned out to be soft and welcoming, the perfect color choice for the room. Vince rolled the color onto the walls quickly to transform the room from storeroom to café. Anne and Lizzie watched as he filled in the corners with a brush. He stood back and looked at his work with a critical eye. Once he painted the moldings and trim it would be perfect.

He turned to face Anne and Lizzie. "What do you think? It just needs some trim and it'll be done."

"Bravo!" Anne clapped as she surveyed the room.

"Ummm, Anne," Lizzie hesitated a minute before continuing. "What do you think about a mural on the back wall? Sorta semi-abstract?" She used her hands to describe a wave breaking on a sea of shells, books, and cannoli.

Anne looked doubtful. Lizzie pulled some scrap paper and a pencil from the front desk and started sketching.

A few minutes later she handed the paper to Anne. "Like this."

Anne's eyes opened wide. In a few elegant lines, Lizzie had swept a world of ocean, books, and food together into an organic whole.

"Lizzie, it's perfect! Absolutely, it's exactly what this room needs. How did you know that?

Lizzie shrugged. "I'm better with pictures than words."

The next day Lizzie sketched pencil lines with an outline of the mural on the mocha sundae wall. "Vince, can you give me a hand with this drop cloth?" He was painting the baseboard on the far side of the room.

They were spreading the canvas on the floor when Vince caught someone peering in the window. By the time he got to the door to scan the sidewalk, it was empty.

"Did you see that guy?"

"What guy?" Lizzie glanced at him. "You mean the one that keeps looking in the window at us?" The hackles rose on Vince's neck and his alarm system moved into high alert.

Could someone have followed Tony and Shirley to Moon Beach? A pit formed in his stomach. How could he have been so reckless to put these innocent people, his new friends, in danger? How could he have stopped watching his back so that he'd know if someone had caught up with him?

"Lizzie, just look at yourself." Anne interrupted Vince's train of thought. "You're gorgeous. If passers-by aren't stopping to take in the view, there's something wrong with them."

Both Lizzie and Vince turned beet red and Anne laughed.

Lizzie snorted. "Y'know, when I catch someone leering, I just start picking my nose. Or something gross like that. You won't believe how fast folks back away when they see that." She shot her dazzling grin at them. "You gotta know how to work with what you've got."

Vince looked at Lizzie. Certainly the sidewalk watcher could have been watching her. Hell, it was hard not to. Vince had to concentrate to keep from looking at her himself sometimes.

But what if the man came looking for Vince?

As it turned out, he was looking for someone else altogether.

# CHAPTER SIXTEEN

"WHAT DO YOU think?" Lizzie held up a colorful poster. She'd drawn a smaller version of the café mural and surrounded it with words announcing the opening reception for the Words & More Café.

"Fantastic!" Anne was enthusiastic.

Lizzie laughed. "Good thing, because I already got a bunch of them printed up." She held up a stack of the glossy posters for Anne. For an instant she looked worried. "Is that all right?"

"All right? It's terrific. They're beautiful. And they're just what we need," Anne said. "Sometimes I forget this bookstore is not the center of everyone's universe. We could use a little 'hey notice me' invitation for folks, both tourists and locals, to come in."

"Really? You and Ernestine are two of the coolest, most inviting people I've ever met. How could anyone not be supportive or interested in what you're doing?"

Anne gave her a long look before speaking. "You'd be surprised, Lizzie."

"Is it all right if I take some posters out and start

spreading the word about this fabulous bookstore run by two cool chicks and the out-a-sight desserts some hot dude is dishing up there?" She pantomimed a cheerleader pose and they both laughed.

"Go for it, my dear. I can't imagine a better advertisement for this, or any, venture than you."

Lizzie did a final cheer and headed for the door.

She sailed head-on into a man standing on the sidewalk just outside the entrance. Posters flew out of her hands in all directions.

"Sorry!" She bent down to pick up the scattered papers. The man walked away without offering to help.

She stared at his back as he trudged down the block. Wasn't he the same guy who'd spent so much time staring in the window when Vince and she were painting?

For days before the opening, Vince barely emerged from the kitchen of the yellow cottage, which turned out to be surprisingly well-outfitted for baking. They were expecting, hoping, that most of the town would show up for the party. He wanted to make sure that there was a good sampling of what he could do. Little pastries filled the refrigerator and tart shells lined the countertop when Ernestine came in for a taste test.

"Free food, of course everyone and his dog'll be there," Ernestine sniffed. "Let's just hope they tell their friends and everyone who visits them to come in when we're open for regular business. Buy some books, buy a rum cake, sit down, and gossip a while." She stuck her finger into a bowl of whipped cream and licked it. "Mmmm. Good stuff."

The day of the opening reception finally arrived. Lizzie

arranged the big display of flowers at the end of the table. She stuck a bloom behind her ear and arranged one in Ernestine's hair and one in Anne's.

"Beautiful!" Bernie said.

"Do they look okay at this end of the table?" Lizzie rearranged individual pieces of ivy in the big vase.

Bernie laughed. "I didn't even notice the table, Lizzie. I was talking about you three lovely ladies."

Anne smiled her crooked smile and Lizzie turned bright red.

Ernestine chuckled and said, "Flattery will get you everywhere, Bernie. Now will you hand me a glass of wine?"

Within minutes, the room was full of people. Lizzie poured little glasses of wine while Vince kept the platters filled with pastries. By the time the mayor, police chief, and what seemed like all the residents of Moon Beach had come through to satisfy both their curiosity and their sweet tooth, the entire bookstore was bustling with laughter and conversation.

Vince noticed the stranger as soon as he walked in the door. He was carrying an expensive leather portfolio and wearing polished wingtips. The combination convinced Vince the man was a crook.

Bernie saw him right away, too. The portfolio and shoes told him the man was a lawyer.

Lizzie also recognized the new guy. It was the asshole who'd been ogling her while she painted the mural.

All three of them were correct in their assessments.

# CHAPTER SEVENTEEN

"WELCOME TO WORDS & More." Anne smiled at the man frowning in front of her. "Would you like something to eat? Drink?"

He didn't bother to smile back as he looked around the room. "I'm looking for Ernestine Castleton. Where is she?"

Ernestine edged forward when she heard her name until she was standing directly in front of the man. "I'm Ernestine. Would you like something to eat? A glass of wine perhaps?" Long years ago, her mother had tried to teach her how to deal with bullies. It rarely worked, but she kept trying. The tactic involved finding an unlikely position of strength and using it.

She picked up a glass of red wine and stuck it in the man's hand. One swipe with her walking stick and she could ruin his crisp white Egyptian cotton shirt with its monogrammed cuffs.

"How can I help you?" She stared straight into his chest as she spoke.

By now, Bernie, Vince, Anne, and Jack had sauntered

over and the police chief was watching with interest from the corner. The man was silent.

"Young man, if you have something to say, say it. We're having a party and quite frankly you are not adding anything to the festivities." She poked her stick against his elbow, jostling it so a little red wine sloshed out of the glass and onto the front of his jacket.

This was not going to be as easy as he had thought. She was supposed to be a pushover.

Charm was not the man's strong suit, but he tried smiling at her belatedly. His cheeks ached from the effort. "I'm here to offer you a deal you won't be able to refuse."

Ernestine snorted. "Who are you? Whatever makes you think I'd deal with you?"

"This." He thrust a paper at Ernestine. Her sea blue eyes opened wide as she read it.

She snorted again. "You still didn't tell me who you are. Manners, young man, manners."

"Vaughn Blankenship. Attorney Vaughn Blankenship."

Ernestine laughed. "I don't know if you're trying to intimidate me or impress me with that attorney crap. Let's just say you're failing at both." This was not going the way Vaughn Blankenship had hoped.

"What could possibly make you think I'd be interested in this ridiculous proposal?" She waved the paper in his face. "You must think I'm senile."

Blankenship had, in fact, been led to believe she was just that, and he was dismayed at the growing realization that she was anything but. Besides, he did not like the looks of the crowd gathering around Ernestine, especially the tall man with the salt and pepper hair. He looked like a lawyer to Blankenship, and that was exactly the kind of person he hoped to avoid.

The man with the salt and pepper hair stepped forward. "I'm Bernard Simpson, Ms. Castleton's attorney."

Blankenship's heart sank. Every lawyer in the state knew Bernie Simpson, at least by reputation. None of them ever wanted to go against him in a courtroom dispute. Simpson was a master at finding every obscure legal loophole that existed and knowing just how far to push, and sometimes cross, the letter of the law to win a case. He fought hard for his clients and rarely lost.

And here he, Vaughn Blankenship, was in some podunk beach town facing a legal legend instead of a senile old lady desperate for cash. He cursed Ernestine's ex-husband for setting him up this way.

"Sonny." Ernestine poked her stick at Blankenship. He was glad he'd already drained his plastic cup. "What on earth would make you think I'd be interested in selling my home to anyone, let alone a weasel like you, for considerably less than its fair market value?"

Blankenship had no answer. According to her ex-husband, Ernestine owned huge tracts of beach land and was sufficiently mentally confused that she would be willing to let all of it go for a song, particularly if she was led to believe the land would be used for something like a giant feral cat resort.

Of course, the land would be used for no such thing, but once the papers were signed, who cared? He'd been savoring the fee he'd receive for these easy transactions. Instead, he found himself nestled between an octogenarian firecracker and a hump-breaking hard-ass lawyer, facing a very different reality.

He watched his hopes dissolve with the poke of Ernestine's psychedelic walking stick.

His client, Stephen Castleton, had fed him a line of hooey. Over the years, Ernestine had bought a lot of property in Moon Beach. She then transferred ownership of a number of these properties into something called the Moon Beach Trust. Stephen assumed she'd done so when she'd been short on cash and desperate, especially since the properties had sold for less than market value. At least that's what he'd told Blankenship.

Supposedly all Blankenship had to do was offer her a pittance for her stake in the properties and she'd leap at the opportunity to line his pockets with a hefty commission. Then he could go after the rest of this Moon Beach Trust, most likely a bunch of local yokels. It should have been a cake walk.

Instead, he had walked into a snake pit. So much for the easy cash he'd been hoping to score on this land deal. And so much for his client. Ernestine's ex-husband was the doddering old fool, not this feisty woman poking him with her cane.

"Blankenship?" Ernestine's voice brought him back to earth. "I assume this was Stephen's bright idea, yes?"

He nodded and looked away from those piercing eyes.

"Am I correct in assuming you will be able to tell him exactly what I think of him, you ,and this ridiculous proposition?"

He nodded again.

"Well then. The police chief, two of her deputies, and my attorney have heard every single word of this conversation." She smiled at him.

"Now get the hell off my property before I have you

arrested for disturbing the peace."

Blankenship stumbled in his haste to leave. Had Ernestine tripped him with her walking stick?

No matter. He was thankful to get away before Bernie Simpson ate him alive. He barely heard the laughter coming from the bookstore behind him as he raced to his car and contemplated his next move.

He never even had the chance to mention the feral cat retirement resort that was supposed to clinch the deal. That was probably just as well.

# CHAPTER EIGHTEEN

BY 6 P.M., the last guest had left. Anne looked at the empty serving plates as they cleaned up the room.

"Well, I guess we don't have to worry about what to do with the leftovers. Vince, you were a real hit today."

"Everyone was a real hit today." Bernie countered as he smiled at his wife. "Let's go home and celebrate."

Back in their big living room, Bernie popped open a bottle of champagne. Anne kicked off her shoes and sank into a deep couch as Lizzie handed her a glass, which she promptly lifted to everyone.

"Here's to us and a successful launch to Words & More's next phase!" Anne smiled as she raised the toast.

"I'm counting on it," Ernestine said. "We had folks come in from up and down the coast. I think a lot of them were surprised to see what our little Moon Beach has to offer. We'd better not be too successful, though. I'd hate to see us change too much."

Anne turned to Vince. "Wasn't that the pastry chef from Geppetto's Restaurant grilling you for the secret to your cream filling? If we're not careful, you're going to be swept into baking for all the Italian restaurants along the coast."

Vince grinned. Was the champagne making him giddy? Or was it something else? Whatever it was, he felt good. "I wouldn't worry about that happening any time soon. Still, it's something to keep in mind. Who knows? Maybe we'll start a 'bake-and-book' enterprise together and take the whole shebang on the road."

"You can never quite tell what the future holds. It's a good idea to keep an open mind for just about anything. And, of course, good friends and a full glass." Ernestine drained her glass. "Lizzie dear, can I trouble you to open another bottle of champagne for us?"

There was silence while Lizzie filled the glasses again.

Bernie raised his glass for another toast. "Here's to Vaughn Blankenship. Poor bastard had no idea who and what he was up against. Ernestine has the sharpest business sense of anyone I know. And the most humanitarian. Definitely not someone to trifle with."

Ernestine shrugged. "It's just a simple equation, whether in business or life. Give. And take. They've got to equal out."

"Ernestine, you're downplaying your genius." Bernie turned to Vince, Jack, and Lizzie. "A couple of bad years hurricane-wise and some folks get spooked and want to move inland. After the area got hit hard two seasons in a row, it was almost impossible to sell anything here. Ernestine paid people more than a fair price for their property so they could move on, or in some cases, stay. She's bought more than one property just as it's headed for foreclosure, and then let folks stay put.

"Now Moon Beach Trust owns prime property all

along the coast. No wonder Blankenship was chomping at the bit! Most people, like our buddy Blankenship, see the word 'Trust' and think 'Bank.' That's the very opposite of trust, in my book."

Ernestine waved Bernie's words aside. "I was lucky I had the little bit of money I had to buy that first property. It's always seemed crazy to me that, once I had a little property, a little money, it became so much easier to pick up more. Way easier than it was for other folks. No wonder Wall Street types can get rich when everyone else struggles.

"Wall Street types don't give back like you do, Ernestine," Anne said. "Moon Beach Trust operates on a different principle. People can live in a Trust house as long as they want or need to, and pay whatever they can. Sometimes it's money, but more often than not they give something else altogether. It's how things work around here."

Ernestine finished her champagne before speaking. "I told you, it's a simple matter of give and take. Take only what you need and give back whatever you can. Totally different than taking whatever you can and giving back the least you can get away with.

"It needs to balance out in the end. Like the ebb and flow of the tide. It's all part of the Moon Beach magic."

She winked at Vince. "I'll bet we could even work some magic on that old man of yours, get him to give a little instead of taking all the time."

Vince wasn't so sure. The tide could rise and fall all it wanted, but it couldn't move a mountain. Ernestine didn't know Tony like he did.

# CHAPTER NINETEEN

"I'VE GOT TO go see him," Vince said.

"You sure that's a good idea?" Jack looked concerned.

"You saw him when he was here. He looked like an old man, and he's only sixty-two. He's aged a lot since we left. Shirley mentioned a heart attack when she was talking to Bernie. I might need to say my goodbyes. Just to get some closure. Tie up loose ends or whatever so I can move on."

"What if he wants you to stay and keep on taking care of him? Can you stand up to him and say no?"

Vince breathed in and savored the freedom he'd experienced since leaving Royal Palm Breeze. His world had grown, and he had grown with it. He thought about leaving Moon Beach and his friends. Friends. Living, breathing people he liked, people who liked him. The bookstore, the café. Could he leave all this behind?

"Thanks to you, and Bernie, the bookstore, all of this," Vince gestured to include the cottages of Whispering Pines. "I can say no to him now. I gave him my all for a long time, and Tony was happy to take it. Maybe if we could meet half-way it would be different. But with Tony it's all or nothing. I'm coming down on nothing this time. But I'd like to end on a positive note if possible."

Vince spent days preparing Tony's favorite foods: sausage lasagna, ricotta pie, spinach manicotti. He flash-froze them to take with him. The day before he left he made Tony a huge tiramisu, heavy with rum and cream on top of homemade ladyfingers. Even Vince the perfectionist thought it was his best effort yet. He hoped Tony would enjoy it.

Jack hovered over Vince as he packed a big cooler with dry ice and opened the trunk of the rental car. There was a pile of old newspapers in the trunk. "You want me to get rid of these?"

"Nah, they might come in handy. Who knows?" They slid the cooler on top of the papers. Vince tossed a duffel bag next to the cooler, slammed the trunk, and slid into the driver's seat.

Jack leaned into the open window when Vince turned the ignition. "You sure you want to do this?"

Vince wasn't, but he felt like he had no choice. "It'll be okay. I've just got to say goodbye to the old man."

"Be careful, my friend," Jack said.

"You too. And keep those chicken suits handy. You never know when you might need them." Vince put the Moon Beach shell Ernestine had given him that first morning on the dashboard for good luck. He adjusted the mirror and headed down the long driveway.

Miles later, Vince examined the baseball caps at the Flying J Plaza. He couldn't decide between the NASCAR and the camo caps, and finally bought both, as well as a pair of white wraparound shades with metallic lenses. What the hell, he grabbed a T-shirt with a Confederate flag on the front and headed back to the car.

Who needed a chicken suit with stuff like this.

# CHAPTER TWENTY

"I'M NOT FEELING so hot today," Tony said.

Shirley looked at him. What a pain in the ass the guy turned out to be. "You look kinda gray. You want some soup or something?" She knew there were a couple of cans in the pantry and the least she could do was open one of them.

"Nah. I just wanna sit for a while. I don't think soup is gonna help my stomach none."

"Whatever." Shirley turned back to *Southern Lifestyles* and continued to flip through the magazine's glossy pages. The pictures from a spa near Miami looked inviting and she began daydreaming about sitting in the hot tub, Margarita in hand.

She heard a car pull into the driveway and looked at Tony. Nobody ever visited them. When the door bell rang, Tony said, "You answer it if you want. I don't feel like getting up."

She peered out the window next to the front door. It was Vince! And he was lugging a big cooler! Shirley nearly danced with joy at the prospect of homemade lasagna. Maybe now that Vince was back, she could figure out her next move.

She yelled, "Tony! Vince is here!" before opening the door and running outside. She grabbed one end of the cooler. "Where the hell you been? It's like you vanished or something."

Tony eased himself out of his recliner and lumbered toward the door. He spied the cooler. Thank heaven Vince was back. He didn't know how much more of Shirley he could take. And he felt queasy, probably could use some home cooking.

"Where the hell you been?"

"Nice to see you too, Dad." Shirley had already opened the cooler and was tearing through the aluminum foil covering the various trays.

"I brought you some food. You want me to heat something up?"

Tony grunted and nodded. "You got lasagna?"

Vince turned the oven on and stuck in the big tray of lasagna. He'd brought soup and poured it into a saucepan so they could eat that while waiting for the lasagna.

Vince shaved pecorino romano into a steaming bowl of minestrone and Tony slurped his way through it.

They still hadn't spoken a word when Vince cut big slabs of lasagna onto plates for all of them. Eventually Tony spoke. "More," he said as he shoved his plate in Vince's direction. For a few minutes, at least, the nausea and tightness had left him as he savored the rich sauce and homemade pasta he'd only dreamed about since Vince left. Vince dished out a second portion of lasagna and passed it back to Tony.

Vince looked at his father and, finally, his father looked

back at him. Their eyes met for a fraction of a second. Tony's lips moved almost imperceptibly into a smile and he mumbled, "*Grazie.*"

Vince felt relieved that he'd been able to give his father the one thing he seemed to want from him. Maybe the trip was worth it after all.

"Save some room for the tiramisu." Vince cut huge slices of the cake and passed them around the table. He went into the kitchen to make the espresso that would set off the sweet richness of the dessert perfectly.

He waited for the water to boil and push its way through the dark coffee grounds.

Shirley focused on her dessert. She plowed through hers until she scraped her plate clean with her fork, then her finger. She was ready for a second piece.

She opened her eyes wide when she finally looked across the table at Tony.

"Vince. I think you better come in here."

The espresso maker drowned her voice out with its one final, loud *sshhhh* and Vince filled three little cups with the dark liquid. He carried the tray into the dining room and looked at his father.

"Holy shit."

Tony was slumped over on his plate of half-eaten tiramisu. His eyes were wide open. He was still smiling.

"I think he's dead," Vince said.

# CHAPTER TWENTY-ONE

VINCE MOVED FAST after he called Tony's doctor. Tony's old cronies could move in with lightning speed when someone in the family died. Vince wanted to make sure he was gone before they arrived.

"Shirley, what'd you do with Tony's ring?" The big diamond pinky ring Tony always wore was missing.

She flashed a weak smile. "I wanted to hold on to it for safe keeping before anyone else took it. You know, like the police or EMS guys. You can't trust anyone these days."

"Shirley, the guy's not cold yet and you're fleecing him. Nice." Vince was disgusted.

"While you're at it, though, you might as well look around the house and see if there's anything else you want to steal." That would keep her out of his hair for a while.

The police and the hearse left at the same time. Another old man, another heart attack. Happened every day. Vince called the funeral home to make arrangements.

"Yes, a simple mahogany casket would be appropriate," he said.

For Chrissakes, it was a cremation. A cardboard box would work. "Yes, bring 'the remains' to the house when they were ready. Someone from the family would be here to receive them." Would they ever.

Vince knew he had little time and much to do. First, he took a shovel to the rose garden they'd put in as a tribute to his mother after she died. It was time to pick up his inheritance.

He drove to the Buy Here, Pay Here car lot just down the street and looked around. The bright blue convertible would work just fine. Minutes later he was on his way back to Royal Palm Breeze with the keys.

Shirley was rooting through Tony's drawers and coming up empty when Vince walked in.

"Shirley, you've got to get out of here. Tony would want me to take care of you, so listen to me." Tony would want no such thing, but Vince needed to make sure Shirley was out of the way in case someone put the heat on her to say where Vince was. She had the Moon Beach address.

Shirley's eyes opened wide as Vince peeled off a substantial wad of bills and handed them to her. "For you to get a fresh start. But you've got to leave now and do what I say."

He handed her the keys to the convertible. "Let's call this your goodbye gift from Tony. I want you to drive to the Buy Here, Pay Here car lot on Broadway. Park the SUV as far from any other vehicles as you can, leave the keys in it and get in the bright blue convertible that's parked on the lot. It's got temporary plates and the paperwork's in the glove box. Then drive out of town. As fast as you can. I'm gonna follow you just to make sure you do that."

Shirley didn't look like she believed Vince, but she got in the SUV. Vince's rental car pulled out of the driveway behind her and minutes later they were both in the lot on Broadway. Shirley pulled the SUV next to the back retention pond and trotted over to the little convertible.

The sun caught the silver metal flake in the car's bright blue paint so it seemed to glow. Shirley looked at her reflection in the side window and smiled. She opened the door and got in the driver's seat.

Vince was saying something, but she'd already turned on the radio and its six speakers drowned out his words. She waved at him as she squealed out onto Broadway toward the highway.

Vince followed her down Broadway for several blocks, then pulled into the Piggly Wiggly parking lot. He put on the wraparound shades, decided on the NASCAR cap and tilted it low on his forehead.

He wanted to take back roads out of town, but thought he'd push his luck just a bit and head back past Royal Palm Breeze for one last look. He was driving down Sandpiper Road when a super-charged black pickup truck passed him on the curve and hung a sharp left, tires squealing, toward the Royal Palm Breeze entrance. In the rear view mirror, he could see another vehicle barreling toward him so he took a quick right onto Swordfish Drive to get out of the way.

He figured he had five minutes at most before they realized what they were looking for was already gone.

That gave him five minutes to hit the road ahead of them and disappear.

# CHAPTER TWENTY-TWO

VINCE DIDN'T LOOSEN his grip on the steering wheel until he crossed the state line heading south. He was exhausted. He wanted to stop for the night, sleep in an anonymous motel room somewhere, sleep away the image of Tony's motionless face framed by whipped cream and chocolate shavings.

Mostly, though, he wanted to get back to Moon Beach and Whispering Pines. Home. He grinned at the realization that, for the first time since his mother had died, he felt he had a home, a place he might actually want to be.

Finally. After all that time kowtowing to his dad, he'd begun to find himself. See some sunlight, some hope. Fresh energy surged through him. Yes, he could certainly drive on through. He wanted to get home.

He wanted, too, to make sure his cargo made it safely back to Whispering Pines and away from the possibility that anyone else would find it. It loomed heavy on his mind and in the trunk of the rental car.

He hoped the Dayton, Ohio newspapers he'd found in

the rental car and left on Tony's kitchen counter would be enough of a lure to send the big black pickup hurtling toward the Rust Belt. Later, maybe, he'd figure out a way to make some waves somewhere far from Moon Beach so Tony's friends would look for him there if they looked at all.

He pulled off the highway and into a Flying J Plaza for gas. After he filled the tank, he parked and went inside to pee.

"This here'll change your life."

"Huh?" Vince looked up at the big guy towering over him. He was holding a small microwave oven, one of hundreds of items on display on the way to the rest rooms. Most of them plugged into your vehicle and claimed they would make long-haul driving and life on the road easier, safer, better.

"Change your life. Make coffee in it whenever you want. Heat up a sausage biscuit, scramble an egg. Tell ya, don't need nobody, nothing else. Gettin' this here baby was better'n findin' Jesus."

In the man's giant paw, the microwave looked like a kid's toy. Certainly not life-changing, but what did Vince know? He still had a lot to learn about life.

"Thanks for the tip. Not today, but I'll keep it in mind for my next trip." The big guy was wearing an impossible Hawaiian shirt, covered with palm trees, surfboards, motorcycles, and beer company logos. He was carrying a couple of cans of Red Bull and some beef jerky sticks.

Vince headed for the refrigerator shelves and grabbed some Red Bull himself. When he got to the checkout he added a bag of peanuts and some M&M's.

A rack next to the cash register displayed T-shirts for a

2008 classic car rally and some faded denim work shirts, all half-price. And one impossible Hawaiian shirt covered with palm trees, surfboards, motorcycles, and beer company logos.

Vince grabbed the Hawaiian shirt and added it to his stash already on the counter. What the hell. He might want a reminder of what life-changing is all about.

As Vince got closer to Moon Beach he spent as much time looking in the rear view mirror as looking straight ahead. Nothing seemed out of the ordinary, but you couldn't be too careful, he thought to himself. He'd been on secondary roads for several hours and saw farm trucks, school buses, and the beefed up Chevys young men with no future spent their money on instead of dental care or higher education. Looked like business as usual to him.

He called Jack. "Hey, can you meet me at the Walmart out near the airport? In an hour and a half? I'll be near the garden shop. Thanks." He hung up before Jack had a chance to say a word.

Vince got there in less than an hour, and spent the extra time surveying the lot in case he was being followed. He wanted to blend in, not have anyone notice him. It was Walmart. He was glad he'd put on the Hawaiian shirt.

Jack pulled up next to the rental car and got out. Vince started in before Jack had a chance to say a word: "Look, can you go in and buy a couple bags of cow manure, then drag them back here on one of those big carts? Two ought to be enough. I don't want to leave the car if I don't have to."

By now, Jack knew Vince well enough to head directly for the garden shop without stopping to talk. Eight minutes later he was back, pushing a cart with eighty pounds of cow manure.

"That's great. Let's get this in first." Vince tossed his duffel bag into the back of the Jeep. "Now let's put these bags on top and get out of here. Drive over to the airport and park in the short-term lot. I'll meet you there as soon as I return the rental car."

Jack finally had a chance to speak as Vince got back in his car. "Nice shirt, buddy."

Vince drove through a warren of warehouses until he saw the purple Ronny's Rentals sign and pulled into the lot. The young woman at the front desk never even looked up from her *People* magazine when Vince walked in with the car rental agreement and the keys. She shoved it all into a pile of paperwork behind her, snapping an enormous wad of pink bubble gum as she did.

He got on the shuttle bus which snaked its way to the terminal. He walked in the building and pretended to look at the flight departure schedules before heading to the men's room. When he came out, he looked around briefly before heading to the exit and the short-term parking lot.

"You see anyone suspicious looking while you were sitting here?" Vince asked as soon as he got in Jack's Jeep.

"What, you mean besides you? What's going on?" Jack backed out of the parking space and headed toward the cashier's booth. "You got any cash? I think it's five bucks."

Vince pulled a wad of bills out of his pocket and handed Jack a twenty. Jack looked at the roll of bills and whistled.

Vince ignored him. He pushed the seat back as far as he could. "Man, it smells like shit in here."

# CHAPTER TWENTY-THREE

SHIRLEY TURNED THE radio up and started punching the dial until she heard Barry Manilow's voice. She crooned "Looks Like We Made It" along with Barry at the top of her lungs.

Shirley felt good. She had made it. She had the car, she had cash, and of course she had her own personal assets. She'd also had the presence of mind to plow through Tony's foul-smelling dog biscuits and pull out a couple of the credit cards with her name on them. She was a survivor and she knew it. The world was a wide-open highway. Shirley and her new convertible were ready to roll down it.

Now she was headed to the Spa at Seacrest for some much-deserved pampering. *Southern Lifestyles* had lavished praise on Seacrest and its glitzy facilities. The pictures in the magazine featured attractive couples golfing, sailing, and eating dinner by candlelight. She was ready. She hoped it wouldn't take her too long to meet someone to share her new life, her new Southern lifestyle.

Shirley pulled into a service plaza for gas. You'd think

Buy Here Pay Here could have topped off the tank. When she got out of the car a sharp pain shot through her left foot and she nearly fell over.

She bent down to see what had knocked her off balance.

Tony's pinky ring. It had slipped out of her pocket and bounced off her foot onto the pavement. When she picked it up, she looked at it closely for the first time.

It was ugly, with that big diamond and the funny markings along the side. She ought to sell the damn thing before she lost it. The diamond alone ought to be worth something.

Shirley picked a pawn shop close to the city center rather than out near the highway, figuring they'd cater to a higher class clientele. Still, she knew she needed all her charm and more than a little sympathy to get the best deal.

She unbuttoned the top two buttons on her blouse and walked into Mr. Earl's Pawn and Gun Shop dabbing her eyes with a tissue and crying softly.

Mr. Earl looked at her with suspicion.

"You gotta help me, help us. My husband, Big Jim, is over at the county hospital with Little Jimbo." Shirley sobbed before continuing. "Little Jimbo! Our baby! The doctors won't do nothing else for him unless we come up with some more money, and we plumb already used every durn penny we had in this world."

Mr. Earl's eyes widened as she reached into her blouse and pulled Tony's ring out from between her breasts. The ring was still warm when she put it in Mr. Earl's hand.

"This here ring is all we got left. It's the only memory we got of Grampa Jim, bless his soul. But if selling it means we can save our baby's life," Shirley racked her brain to remember the baby's name, "then we'll get rid of everything we got. Grampa Jim'd understand.

"Please. Little Jimmy only has a few hours left. You gotta help us save him."

Shirley grabbed Mr. Earl's hand across the counter and pressed it suggestively.

In his line of work, Mr. Earl had seen and heard just about everything. He didn't believe most of it, and with good reason. He could tell Shirley was lying as soon as she got out of her shiny new car.

But this ring was something special and he knew it, even if she didn't. He recognized those markings and they scared him.

They haggled over price until Mr. Earl finally handed Shirley a wad of bills and a pawn ticket.

He was on the phone before she even got back to her car.

# CHAPTER TWENTY-FOUR

JACK PULLED INTO the long winding driveway to Whispering Pines, headlights leading the way. Home. Vince was almost giddy with relief and with the calm that home conjured to him.

Jack got out of the car and started up the steps. "You want a beer? You must be beat after all you've gone through since you left. I'm exhausted just listening to your story."

"In a minute. I've got to take care of something first."

Jack sat out on the deck and waited. He could hear Vince rumbling around in the underbrush. A shovel hit dirt and eventually the distinctive odor of Pure Gold cow manure wafted up to the deck. Then Vince came up the stairs and went into the cottage. Jack could hear the shower running.

Five minutes later, Vince came outside with two cold beers. He handed one to Jack and sat down.

"Thanks." Jack paused before asking, "You think Shirley's out of the picture for good?"

"Yeah, I think so. She was reading one of those 'best

places for single women to live and find happiness and men' articles in some glossy magazine right before Tony keeled over. I'll bet she's on her way to one of them now.

"It broke my heart to give her that much money and the car and all. Still, it's cheap if it means she's gone. I just hope she finds herself another sucker before she blows through all that cash."

Vince thought for a minute before continuing.

"She could possibly get herself into some trouble, though."

"How so?"

"Tony had this diamond pinky ring he wore all the time. It was sort of a family heirloom. Shirley ripped it off him as soon as the poor guy stopped breathing. Fine by me, I sure didn't want it or anything to do with it." Vince took a long drink from his beer.

"But if she ever decided to pawn the ring it could get ugly for her. I tried to warn her when she got in the damn convertible, but she was so excited to take off she wouldn't listen to me."

A quick image of Shirley waving from the blue car flashed in front of Vince. "You know something?"

"What?"

"Here's the craziest thing. Shirley's a pain in the ass, but if it wasn't for her, I'd probably still be in Royal Palm Breeze waiting on Tony hand and foot and watching my life drain away," Vince said. "My life is better now than I ever thought it would be or could be. I can't believe it, but I've got Shirley to thank for that."

Jack was quiet for a minute. "I know what you mean. After Janet died, I just moped around the house and did nothing to help myself. I couldn't snap out of my slump.

Then Shirley showed up and, man, trying to get her out of my hair sure got me off my butt."

They sat looking out at the stars. Crickets and bullfrogs competed for air space, with an occasional *hoot hoot* from the wood owls. In the distance, the surf provided a muted backdrop to the rest of the night sounds.

A hundred, maybe five hundred, miles away that same night sky, those same stars, were pierced by a sudden loud explosion. Shards of bright blue, heavy metal flake steel shot through the air. A pawn ticket from Mr. Earl's flew up in the sky, then floated slowly back down to the pavement where tiny pieces of the little convertible lay scattered in the smoky haze.

Jack looked at Vince. "You hear something?"

"Maybe. Thunder?"

"Dunno. There wasn't any lightning."

They sat in silence a while longer. Then Vince raised his bottle, tapped Jack's in a toast and grinned. "Here's to Shirley," he said.

Jack took a long swig and set his bottle down. "To Shirley."

They both settled back and enjoyed the dark, the peace, the crickets, the sound of the waves.

A shooting star sped across the night sky.

# CHAPTER TWENTY-FIVE

BLANKENSHIP'S HEAD WAS throbbing. What a shithole week this had been. Bad enough the Castleton woman was no dummy, but for him to discover, too late, that she had teamed up with Bernie Simpson was the crap icing on a dung heap cake filled with bad luck.

Well, he wasn't going to let them get away with this. The old lady might own that beachfront property now, but he knew he could make a killing if it belonged to him.

And it was going to belong to him, Bernie Simpson be damned. He couldn't wait to kick that pompous blowhard right out of his wingtips. And the Castleton woman right out of her little cottage.

He, not his ex-client Steven Castleton, was going to own that land. And it was going to make him rich. No matter what it took.

Blankenship gripped the steering wheel as a jagged line broke across his field of vision. Great, all he needed now was a migraine. That prospect and the burning sensation in his gut pushed his bad mood to the edge of its danger zone.

He tried to will the migraine away by concentrating on the god-awful lyrics wafting up through the static on the radio. Guns. Trucks. Cheating women. Damn, couldn't these backwoods idiots come up with something better than this crap?

Should have bought himself an iPod and put some decent stuff on it. Old school, maybe a little Neil Diamond, for driving through the boondocks like this.

Something moved on the road ahead and an almost imperceptible smile broke across Blankenship's face. Maybe the day wouldn't be a total loss after all. He accelerated and aimed directly for the big snapping turtle lumbering across the middle of the road in front of him.

A livestock truck swung wide as it pulled into the curve ahead of him. Blankenship's eyes widened when he heard the truck's air horn blast and saw the big  front grill heading directly toward him.

"Motherfucker!" Blankenship over-corrected and swerved onto the gravel shoulder. The truck's failing brakes and load of pigs squealed in alarm and the truck shot past him. Blankenship's right front tire veered dangerously down into the drainage ditch and he swung a hard left to try to bring the car back up on the shoulder. His shoulders slammed into the seat back as he stood on the brake pedal to stop the car.

He saw a mixture of blue exhaust and road dust in the rear view mirror as the overloaded livestock truck rumbled down the pavement. Plus, the frigging turtle had crossed onto the gravel shoulder and was heading safely down into the drainage ditch.

The same drainage ditch where his car was now stuck. Life sucked sometimes.

The adrenalin rush from nearly flattening himself against a load of bacon went straight to Blankenship's gut. He groaned and willed the migraine to move in and take his mind off his stomach. A wave of nausea hit and the horizon shifted. He would have doubled over from pain if the steering wheel hadn't caught him as he bent over. Stars danced across the dashboard before his vision faded to black.

"Hey, git stuck, huh?"

Blankenship looked up. He must have conked out for a minute. A face peered at him in the side window and the smell of stale cigarette smoke triggered more nausea. Where did this guy come from?

"Y'alls wheels dug inna dirt. Bitch to git outa."

Blankenship tried to shake the fuzziness out of his head and focus on the man peering in his window. Another figure stood behind the man doing the talking. Together they had maybe twenty teeth. He wondered if he should pull his gun out from under the front seat.

"Me 'n Tiny'll give ya a push. Be jes enough to git her goin' agin."

Blankenship looked at the two men. Tiny weighed at least 300 pounds and looked like he could singlehandedly hurl Blankenship's car into the next county. The man talking weighed half what Tiny weighed, but he was sinewy with muscles that appeared hard from a life of outdoor work.

Blankenship nodded. He sure as shit couldn't get out of the ditch on his own.

"Put 'er in low and give 'er some gas when I tell ya." Tiny hitched up his pants and walked to the back of the car, tossing his cigarette butt in the ditch as he moved. "C'mon, Lloyd."

The two men braced themselves and grabbed the rear bumper. Tiny shouted the directions: "Hidey Hidey HO! Hidey Hidey HO!"

It took Blankenship two HOs to figure out that was when he should step on the gas. On the third HO, the left front wheel grabbed the gravel and the car eased out of the ditch.

He would have kept going but the two men's big pickup truck blocked his way. Blankenship went on alert. Why would these two rednecks stop if they didn't want something from him? He was trapped, here in what he knew was dangerous territory. Was that banjo music he heard in the distance? Blankenship reached down for his gun.

"Yer good to go," Tiny said as the two men walked back to their truck and opened the doors. Blankenship could hear and see an excited flurry of three, maybe four, little yap-yap dogs jumping around when the men climbed up to the cab. Lloyd made kissy noises back at the dogs.

Tiny waved as he pulled onto the road. His beefy upper arm featured a tattooed likeness of the little dog that was already leaning out the truck window to catch the breeze.

"Have a blessed day."

Blankenship stared at the big Confederate flag flying from the back of the pickup as it sped off. He just couldn't figure out these backwoods low-lifes. He put his Glock back under the front seat for the time being, in easy reach. Never know when he might need it for real.

He gasped as another spasm roiled his stomach. It was time for him to do something about his gut, and he hoped he could find some relief out here in the middle of nowhere. He pulled back onto the road.

# CHAPTER TWENTY-SIX

BLANKENSHIP HIT THE turn signal and slowed down when he saw a sign for Main Street. He pulled onto a pitted two-lane road that had once been the main commercial district of the tired little town. Now, the new state highway offered an easy fifteen mile drive to the nearest Walmart and effectively shuttered local businesses.

Main Street, my ass. Pawn shops, auto parts stores, and rusty for rent signs dotted the small strip malls lining both sides of the roadway. The white sand beaches and salt air only a dozen miles away seemed part of a different and distant world.

Blankenship drove slowly down the main drag, looking carefully in each little strip mall for relief. His stomach burned hot enough that he was ready to settle for anything to douse the flames, even if it meant a fast food burger and a soft drink he'd regret within five minutes of swallowing it.

He drummed his fingers impatiently on the steering wheel as he tailgated a slow-moving minivan. This podunk town was the pits and a waste of his time. Not even a Mickey D's.

Jackpot. And not a minute too soon. Nature's Best Health Foods sat crammed in between a second-hand shop and a storefront church proclaiming "The Bible is a better guide than your TV Guide" on its hand-painted marquee. He swerved into the parking lot, pulled into a handicap spot, and got out of the car.

He hated health food stores. The thought of patchouli oil, granola, and geezers wearing Birkenstocks made his gut clench up even more than it had in the car. He groaned as he approached the door.

"You okay, man?" A bearded man wearing an Eat More Broccoli! T-shirt opened the door for him.

Blankenship grunted and headed inside. Probiotics. Sounded like voodoo to him but when the receptionist with the big tits at his doctor's office had said she swore by the stuff as the holy grail for victims of gut-wrench, he figured it was worth a try. Damn sight cheaper than sitting in a doctor's office breathing other people's germs and slathering himself with hand sanitizer.

The receptionist had seemed a hell of a lot healthier than the doctor, with his nicotine stained teeth and bad breath. The second the doctor opened his mouth, Blankenship stood up and left the office. He didn't have many standards, but a doctor who smoked was off his list.

He'd even remembered to thank the receptionist for the tip on his way out the door. It gave him a minute to ogle her stack before he left.

He hated to admit it, but he felt better after taking the voodoo stuff for the first time, even though it tasted like crap to him. Too bad he had to walk into a health food store to get his fix.

These little hippy dippy stores were all arranged differently and he never knew where to look for the stuff he wanted. Plus the whole damn store was covered with green posters making it next to impossible for him to find anything. He doubled over with pain and groaned to himself, cursing Steven Castleton and the false hopes he'd engendered about Ernestine's property and his own future.

When Blankenship straightened back up, he saw the familiar probiotics bottle directly in front of him. Finally. He grabbed one, added an overpriced bottle of water, and headed for the checkout line.

"You going to the Green Alliance Fair?" The cashier moved in slow motion, chatting with the customer in front of him like they were old friends. Blankenship drummed his fingers on the checkout counter and willed the two men to move faster.

"Wouldn't miss it, man." The bearded broccoli T-shirt stood directly in front of him with a bag of nuts and some fruit. "That is the best showcase for what's happening with the green movement around the country. Just hope we can get more of that going on around here. Be great to build some awareness about the environment. We could sure use more money coming into the area, too. Especially money built around sustainable stuff. I'm sick of these big beach houses on steroids and developers who don't give a damn about nature."

The cashier nodded. "Totally. About time something besides shopping malls, high-rise condos, and mini-mansions cropped up to take over what's left of the coast. Too bad the wildlife around here can't speak for itself, y'know?"

Blankenship shuffled his feet impatiently while they talked and finally waved his credit card in the cashier's face.

The cashier swiped the card and handed it back. "You need a bag for this stuff?"

Blankenship nodded. What a dipshit. Of course he needed a bag. Did they expect him to walk out of the frigging store carrying the bottles like a damn shoplifter?

"Have a nice day." The cashier was already ringing up the next customer's order with one hand as he stuffed a flyer in Blankenship's bag next to his Probiotics Promise.

Blankenship sat in the car gulping his probiotics fix and the bottled water from half-way around the world, waiting impatiently for instant relief. He'd already guzzled down most of the water when he pulled the green flyer out of the grocery bag.

Blankenship read through the Green Alliance Fair announcement and forgot all about his aching stomach.

Glory hallelujah! He might have just found religion. Maybe it would turn out to be a good day after all.

The Green Alliance, according to the flyer, consisted of dozens of organizations focused on saving the environment throughout the coastal South. Some of the organizations had a national sphere as well. Blankenship had always thought the do-gooders' save-the-baby-animals mentality was a bunch of crap, but as he looked at the flyer, an idea began forming in his twisted mind.

Some of these groups actually had a substantial amount of money and power. And they were looking for backers. What's more, they had credibility, something Blankenship lacked.

If only Ernestine's land were in his grasp! Possibilities

for its abuse and misuse swam into his brain with a speed that gratified him as he scanned the flyer. There had to be a way for him to take advantage of the opportunities this Green Alliance schtick had to offer. The Alliance might just provide the leverage he needed to get his hands on Ernestine's property. It certainly was worth a try.

Perhaps the Green Alliance Fair was a sign that his luck was changing, and fate was giving him a second chance if only he played his cards right.

Unfortunately, he would need to do some actual work if he wanted something to happen. He looked at the date for the upcoming Green Alliance Fair. There wasn't much time. But if he hustled it might be enough. He headed back toward the highway.

Maybe, just maybe, he could come up with a viable plan before the fair. Already his stomach felt much better.

# CHAPTER TWENTY-SEVEN

VINCE STRETCHED HIS left leg out straight against the walkway railing, feeling resistance in his hamstring as he did so. He inhaled the morning air, fragrant with sweet acacia and salt. He repeated the hamstring stretch with his right leg, then he headed toward the sound of the waves.

Vince found running along the hard-packed sand at the water's edge exhilarating. His thoughts blew out in all directions as he ran down the beach accompanied by a band of pelicans flying low above the water.

As he got into the rhythm of his run, his mind calmed and he focused on the steady movement of his body, his footfalls on the sand. This early in the morning he could run for miles and not see a soul. Even when he ran later in the day he'd see only a few people, perhaps a mother building sand castles with a couple of small children or someone stretched out in a beach chair, engrossed in a paperback book.

Thirty minutes into his run he stopped to strip off his soaked T-shirt. He wiped the sweat from his forehead and swept the shirt over his head, trying to tame the damp black hair that kept falling into his face. He stuffed the T-shirt into the back waistband of his running shorts, leaned into a quick stretch and began running again, the salt air blowing on his bare chest.

Eventually he turned and started to run back toward Whispering Pines. The prospect of fresh coffee and the blueberry muffins he'd made the night before made him smile as he began his slower, cool-down run.

"Good morning, my friend." He heard a voice behind him.

Vince whirled around and saw Ernestine walking down a path through the dunes. She was holding a travel mug in one hand and her walking stick in the other. He watched as she sat down on a weathered bench at the end of the path and patted the spot beside her.

"Care to join me for a spell?"

"I'm afraid I'm pretty sweaty," he said and remained standing.

Ernestine looked at Vince's long, lean body and chuckled. "There's nothing wrong with good, honest sweat, young man. But if you prefer to stand there where I can see you better, go right ahead. I may be an old lady but I can still appreciate some decent scenery." She took a long drink without taking her eyes off Vince's chest.

Vince was already red from exertion so his blush went unnoticed. He quickly changed the subject. "Moon Beach sure is a nice place to run," he said.

"Oh, that it is. It's a grand place for many things. I hope you don't mind if I ask you a question."

She didn't give him a chance to respond as she continued. "I'm wondering, are you still running away?" She caught Vince's blue eyes with her own and held them without blinking. She waited.

"I don't know," he said after a long pause. "Running along Moon Beach is a new experience for me. I used to run on a treadmill in my dad's garage until I was exhausted. Kind of like a hamster on one of those wheels in a cage. Maybe hamsters love that kind of thing, but I sure didn't. I hated running on that treadmill and never getting anywhere." Vince stopped for a minute. He wasn't used to talking that much, or having anyone listen.

"So, yeah, I guess I'm still running away from that. And from the question of how I let myself get stuck in a rut for so long." He shook his head.

"Tony–that's my dad–and I both freaked out when Mom died. Tony, for all his faults, really loved her, I think. Maybe he just couldn't handle being alone and that's why he grabbed onto me so hard. But I'm not sure why I let him," he said.

"It's nice to be able to run straight along the shoreline now instead of around in circles, that's for sure."

"Any idea what you're running toward?"

He shook his head again. "Not a clue."

Ernestine looked at him. This time she focused on his legs. "Give it time, Vince. Give it time." She took another sip from her mug and stood up. "Eventually you'll know." She turned and headed back toward the dunes.

Vince watched until she was out of sight. He thought more about her words. For the first several weeks in Moon Beach, he had felt like he was running away, but as each footfall hit the sand he could feel a tiny bit of his past slip away. He only wished he had the answer to Ernestine's last question.

He walked slowly along the beach and then down the

walkway toward the Whispering Pines Cottages, each step making a hollow sound against the wooden slats. When he got to the end of the walkway, he rested his hands on his hips and arched backward, stretching enough that he looked straight up into the sky, bright blue as the day began in earnest.

Lizzie loved this time of day. Even when she slept poorly, as she had last night, the morning offered a fresh start.

Especially now. She looked out the window toward the beach walkway. She cradled her mug of coffee as she watched him, stretching in slow motion against the railing. He was damp with sweat, and his muscles shone as the early morning sunlight streamed across his body. She inhaled the steam from her coffee and smiled. What a way to start a day.

# CHAPTER TWENTY-EIGHT

VINCE JUMPED WHEN he heard the door slam behind him. He turned around to see Lizzie standing in the hallway.

"Whoa, don't you knock any more?"

"Do I need to? I mean, this is like your office or something, isn't it?"

He stared at her. She was backlit by the sun through the kitchen window and her hair gleamed copper.

"Listen, you're like a madman racing around the kitchen all the time. You could use some help in here," Lizzie said. "Tell me what to do and I'll do it. I used to bake cookies and stuff with my mom all the time and so I probably won't blow up things. At least not here."

She smiled. "Why are you staring at me like that?"

Vince looked away and shook that flaming red image to the back of his head. He definitely could use some help; Lizzie was right about that. He pointed to a big bag of flour. His own hands were already covered with sticky dough. "You want to scoop up a cup of that and start sprinkling it in the bowl when I say to? That'd be great."

Lizzie grabbed the cup and stuck it in the flour. "Do you use a recipe for this stuff?"

"I used to start with one, but a lot of it, maybe it's hocus pocus. I can just feel when the dough is right. It can change with the temperature or humidity or who knows what. You know how you can just feel when something is right?" He noticed for the first time how green her eyes were. "I don't know what it is really. Maybe chemistry."

"Chemistry?"

"Yeah, chemistry. Okay, just start sprinkling the flour in the bowl now."

Lizzie leaned over and slowly started sprinkling flour in circular motions into the big ceramic mixing bowl.

Vince stirred the flour into the mixture until the wooden spoon hit the right amount of resistance. "That's it. Okay, that's enough."

Vince glanced at Lizzie. She'd only been in the kitchen five minutes and already her hair was flecked with flour. There was a dab of dough on her chin and tentatively he reached out to wipe it off.

"Vince!" Her shouting startled him and he recoiled. "The stove!"

He turned as the smell of burning sugar hit him. He grabbed a dish towel and pulled the pot off the stove. Too late! He poured water into the pot and watched as steam hissed out, along with a tantalizing smell.

"Damn! I forgot all about the stove. I guess I ruined it." Maybe having Lizzie here was a mistake. He was used to working alone. He certainly wasn't able to concentrate on his cooking when she was standing there, just inches away. Still with the dough on her chin.

"I don't know, Vince. Whatever's in that pot smells

fantastic, if you ask me. Looks awful, though. What is it?"

"I was caramelizing sugar. You're supposed to melt the sugar real slow. I thought I could do something else while I was waiting for it to melt. I blew it."

"Wait a minute. Burnt sugar cake is some kind of big southern deal. People fight over whose burnt sugar cake is the best at the church picnic and stuff like that. I wonder if you could figure out some kind of burnt sugar and ricotta filling? Southern Italian or something? You know how fusion is hot in cooking now? Where you mix up the unexpected and add a regional flair and all that?" Lizzie was talking fast, too fast, and each question ended with an unnatural inflection. Vince could hardly keep up with her.

"This could be your signature piece. Not that you need anything like that. I mean, your stuff is already awesome. But adding the whole burnt sugar thing would make it crazy good, even better than it already is."

She finally stopped to take a breath, then started back in again. "So what do you think?"

"About what?" Vince was lost.

"About the burnt sugar filling, silly. Really, it could be a knockout. I think you ought to go for it. Words & More could become famous. You could become famous."

Fame was the last thing Vince wanted or needed.

Still, he spent the next several days huddled over the stove, experimenting with different ways to create burnt sugar magic for his creamy fillings. Lizzie tasted each variation with the serious attention of a wine critic.

If he could come up with a breakout item to bring more folks into the bookstore, he knew it would help. He'd seen Anne scowling over the bills and he thought the shop was struggling. Jack had confirmed that when he first looked over the financial accounts.

"What do you think of this one?" Vince asked as soon as Lizzie walked into his kitchen one morning. He already knew that he'd finally gotten the consistency exactly where he wanted it, the sweetness factor just right. Still, he enjoyed watching her as she let the filling glide across her tongue. She licked her lips. Chemistry indeed.

"That's it. Bingo. This is the one, Vince." She dipped her finger into the bowl and scooped out another taste. "Oh, good lord. This is definitely perfection in a mouthful. Sweet Jesus, bless your heart, slap your mama, and all that. Come on, let's fill up some of your cannoli shells and do a test run at the book store."

"Ta Da!" Lizzie announced as she opened the lime green door of Words & More so Vince could walk in with the tray of cannoli. "We are proud to introduce Vince Fantozzi's latest and greatest dessert masterpiece. Come and get it!"

Anne looked up from her paperwork as Vince stopped in front of her with the tray. She tried the burnt sugar ricotta cannoli, its crisp shell oozing with creamy filling. The shell cracked as she bit into it and the filling dissolved into her taste buds.

"Oh, my. Vince, this is the most decadent treat I have ever eaten."

Lizzie nodded. "Sex on a plate," she said. Vince stared at her.

The half-dozen customers in the store looked up after Lizzie spoke. Vince walked over to them and passed around the tray of pastries. Within minutes, the tray was empty.

"You, sir, are a genius." An elderly customer bowed his

bald head before Vince. Then he turned to Lizzie: "And you, young lady, are absolutely correct in your assessment. You have both just made my day. *Congratulazioni!*"

Vince grinned.

Sex on a plate indeed.

# CHAPTER TWENTY-NINE

ANNE AND BERNIE stood leaning against the deck railing before turning in to face each other. Their kiss was long, longer than seemed possible to those watching from the shadows below.

"Oh my god," Lizzie whispered when she could breathe again. "That is so incredible. They are so incredible. They just seem made for each other."

Ernestine chuckled. "Well, yes. They are made for each other. But I've known them both for a long time. In many ways, they made each other."

"What do you mean?"

"You keep anything drinkable in that miniature kitchen of yours?"

Lizzie nodded in response to Ernestine's question.

"Well, then. Let's head inside. Pour me a glass and I'll tell you a story."

Lizzie held up two wine bottles, a white and a red. Ernestine pointed to the pinot noir. "Best heart medicine there is. Well, that and a love story like Anne and Bernie's."

She settled into her chair and watched Lizzie pour two glasses of the ruby liquid. She took a long slow sip before starting to talk.

"Bernie'd just graduated law school and was working out of the public defenders' office. He thought he was the sharpest nail in the toolbox. He was brash and a loud mouth, with no idea when to keep the damn thing shut. It's a miracle he didn't end up at the bottom of a landfill. Then one day real trouble walked into his office."

Ernestine shook her head. "I don't think Bernie had any idea what he was in for when Anne stormed in, too young, too fierce, too beautiful. All alone. And still in shock over what had happened to her."

She sighed. "Poor Anne. If only she'd met Bernie or me or someone who cared before she had her baby, things might have turned out different. She'd been led to believe she could have some ongoing contact with her child–pictures, visitation."

Ernestine swept her hands out in front of her. "Instead, she got nothing. As soon as Anne signed the adoption papers, that baby was gone from her forever. As far as she knew, the family dropped off the face of the earth."

"Oh!" Lizzie turned pale.

"That wasn't even the worst of it. Her delivery had been perfectly normal. She was a healthy sixteen year old. But they'd tied her tubes right after the baby was born."

When Ernestine said this, Lizzie splashed wine on the table. She rose to get a dish towel and instead stood in front of the sink, staring out the window into the darkness.

Ernestine kept talking. "Well. Anne was ready to take on the whole state. The adoption system and the entire hospital industry. And Bernie thought he was a hot enough shit to be able to handle them all."

"Was he? Were they?" Lizzie turned back to face Ernestine.

Ernestine shook her head. "Nah. Bernie's tougher than a two dollar steak, but he was way too inexperienced back then to take on the system and the network of good ole' boys running the state. Their malpractice case got thrown out of court."

"That was it? How could she handle that? I think she would've been a terrific mother."

Ernestine nodded. "It was a terrible loss all around. But the whole ordeal made Bernie the lawyer he is today, willing to go as far out on a limb for justice as the limb's breaking point. And sometimes beyond, if that's what it takes to win." Ernestine pointed to the wine bottle and watched as Lizzie refilled both glasses.

She took a sip and went on. "Anyhow, Anne lived with me while she finished her G.E.D. and then got into a special accelerated program at State. They were so busy with this case and with her in school that it took them until she finished at State for them to look, really look at each other, and finally realize, well, bless my heart! This is love!

"They're a formidable team, all right. They reflect each other's light and the result is what you see. Dazzling, no?"

Lizzie nodded. She ached with sadness for Anne and her lost baby. The image of Anne and Bernie kissing in the dark filled her with longing. Would she ever be able to reflect someone else's light and love the way they did? Given the mess she had left behind before coming to Moon Beach, that seemed an impossibility to her. She felt lost and alone, surrounded by jagged rough edges of her own making.

Ernestine broke into her concentration. "When's your birthday?"

Lizzie told her the date.

"Taurus, eh? You and Anne's daughter both. So you're about two weeks older than her."

Tears filled Lizzie's eyes. She missed her Sunday phone calls with her mother, missed the silly letters they sent each other, filled with stick figure cartoons and love. How must Anne feel? She never had the chance to tell her only child she loved her, to hear the words repeated back to her.

"Ernestine, I'm glad you were there to catch Anne."

"Me too. That's really what it's all about, isn't it? We're all roaming around this earth together and we'd better act like we care about each other. You know what I mean?"

Lizzie nodded. She'd experience the truth behind Ernestine's words sooner than she ever expected.

# CHAPTER THIRTY

VINCE KNEADED THE fragrant dough into a pliable mass. He loved the peaceful calm that accompanied working with dough and the lazy mental drift that came from the rhythmic kneading as the dough became more plastic and easy to shape into small rounds. Zen dough, he thought, and his mind emptied. In some ways, it was like running.

He looked up, startled by the sound in the doorway. Lizzie was leaning against the door frame in the sunlight.

"How long have you been standing there?"

"Um, Vince, do you have any sprinkles?"

"Sprinkles?"

"You know, those little candy things you put on cupcakes or ice cream."

"You mean jimmies?" He opened a cupboard and pulled out a plastic tub filled with tiny chocolate pellets.

"You want some?" He turned back and looked at her. Her face was splotchy and her eyes swollen. "You okay?"

"You ever think about your mother?" Lizzie's question seemed to come out of nowhere.

"Sure I do. Why?"

"Does it ever get easier? I mean, I miss my mom so much. It's really hard not to think of making cookies and her letting me put so many sprinkles on top of a cookie that I couldn't hardly see it. And Anne..." She choked when she mentioned Anne's name.

Lizzie grabbed a ricotta tart from a big platter and covered it with chocolate sprinkles.

She swallowed hard and held the tart in both hands, tilting it to spread the chocolate evenly. "What was your mother like?"

Vince paused for a long time before speaking.

"When I was little, Tony used to hang out with a whole series of different characters. There was Uncle Sal, Uncle Mario, Uncle Jimmy. They weren't really my uncles. Tony called them his business partners. But they were thugs, just like Tony."

He reached into a drawer and pulled out a roll of waxed paper. He covered the dough with a piece of waxed paper and sat down facing Lizzie.

"Once in a while one of these guys would show up at the house at night. When that happened, my mom would rush me up the back stairs and into my room. Then she'd sneak a tray of cookies and milk in and we'd sit in my bedroom with the door closed. I could hear Tony and whatever uncle it was talking downstairs while I played with my trains, and Mom would sit in her rocker and knit."

"The cookies and milk sound just like my mom. Not the rest of it, though."

"Sometimes the voices downstairs would get louder and angrier. When that happened, my mom would fish out this skeleton key she wore on a ribbon around her neck and lock the bedroom door and turn out the light. It was time to play ghost, she'd say, and we needed to be quiet as ghosts. I'd tiptoe into bed in the dark and she'd whisper stories to me until I fell asleep. That's what she was like."

"Wow, she sounds amazing. Were you scared? Was she scared?"

"She was probably scared to death for both of us, but she always made me feel safe, protected. After one of those arguments, the only thing for certain was that we would never see that uncle again. People didn't mess with Tony.

"I thought about that a lot when she was sick. That's when I went back to live with my folks and help out. Tony put a hospital bed in the dining room and I'd sit there in that same rocking chair. I'd feed her ice chips and read to her. Man, did I wish I could make her feel safe! I don't know if she could even hear me by then, but I read all those old stories to her anyway. Dr. Doolittle, Wizard of Oz, all of them, just in case. It was funny, but somehow it made me feel a little better."

He wiped his cheeks with some crumpled waxed paper.

"And she just faded away. I watched her turn into a real ghost right in front of me. It wasn't at all like our game had been.

"Does it get easier? I don't know. I guess if you have a lot of good memories it's got to be super hard. Your mom sounds pretty special, just like mine was. But it's hard no matter what. I mean, I even feel bad about Tony, and he wasn't exactly a model parent."

Vince shook the remaining sprinkles on the rest of the ricotta tarts and pushed the platter to the middle of the table. They sat there without speaking until every crumb and sugar confection was gone.

# CHAPTER THIRTY-ONE

THE POSSIBILITIES OF the Green Alliance dangled before Blankenship like a shiny lure on a sharp hook and he was aching to bite. He was hit with a rare burst of self-awareness as he realized he'd moved too quickly after meeting Steven Castleton. Snatching the Moon Beach properties from a doddering old lady sounded easy. Too easy, if he'd been honest with himself. But greed has a way of altering perceptions and making reality look vastly different than it is.

He had depended solely on Steven Castleton for his initial information and walked into his meeting with Ernestine—and that pitbull Simpson—totally unprepared.

He'd been hoping to grab the Moon Beach properties for a song. Castleton had led him to believe that the original paperwork for the properties was deficient, and his reasoning seemed plausible. These yokels didn't keep records the same way civilized northerners did. And Ernestine herself was supposed to be a pushover.

That she was anything but a pushover was Blankenship's first disappointment. But he held out hope that the rest of her ex-husband's assertions had been correct.

It was now up to him to do the drudge work necessary to find out exactly what yokels' paperwork looked like. His heart sank with the realization that he'd need to invest his own time and energy.

Blankenship found real work boring, and he regretted not having a lackey to plow through the dusty records in the county office for him. Not that he would have been willing to share any positive results the research might have uncovered with anyone else. He'd tried in the past to hire assistants to do his grunt work for him, but for one lame reason or another they'd always quit.

So Blankenship found himself alone, climbing the steps to the county building in Anderton. He hated these old buildings; they were dusty and he never knew what kinds of creepy crawly things were lurking inside. The library and the county offices were crammed into the same small building.

"May I help you?"

At least there was a real person at the library reference desk. Maybe she'd do the work for him.

"I need to find some old property records. Maybe you can find them for me." His mouth hurt as he tried to smile.

The reference desk phone rang and the woman mouthed "Hold on" to Blankenship as she picked up the receiver. She answered interminable questions about tenants' rights for the caller. She even pulled a book from the reference shelf and read from it into the receiver while Blankenship stood there waiting, drumming his fingers along the edge of the oak desk. Finally she hung up and looked at him.

"I'm sorry. What with all our budget cuts, I'm the only one here on Tuesdays and Thursdays. I can show you where the records are filed and then you're welcome to go through them yourself."

Blankenship frowned. "That's the best you can do?"

She stared at him. "Yes it is, as a matter of fact. Do you want to look at what we have or not?"

He nodded and followed her as she got up and walked down the hallway, stopping in front of a door with *RECORDS* written in gold leaf across the glass pane. She opened the door and snapped on an overhead light.

"These ledgers contain the chronological record of all property transactions in the county," she said, pointing to thick books filed on metal shelves.

"Copies of the original deeds are filed chronologically here, in these files." She pointed to stacks of record boxes. "The deeds have the book and page number from the ledgers so you can cross-reference the transactions. We're trying to store all these records digitally in case of fire or another flood, but we're so short staffed it's impossible to make much headway with that."

As if on cue, the reference desk phone began ringing and she turned to leave the room. "If you need to make some copies, I can do that for you at the reference desk. Let me know if you need anything else."

Blankenship looked around in disgust before pulling down one of the heavy leather ledgers. He began wheezing and knew that he'd better work quickly while he could still breathe. He began sifting through records, beginning with the dates Steven Castleton had given him when they first met. Each time a slender silver bug crawled across the yellowed ledger pages, Blankenship shuddered with aversion.

But the thought of besting Bernie Simpson motivated him almost as much as his greed did and so he fought off his irrational fear of the insects, of all wildlife, really. If he allowed himself to panic, his whole body would break out in angry hives. He knew he should carry around one of those EpiPens the doctor had once given him so he could poke himself with it in case he swelled up, but the thought of jabbing himself with a needle didn't appeal to him much either. He'd just try to take deep breaths and keep his mind on what he'd come to do in the first place.

There was a method to this research, he knew, and all he needed to do was work slowly and carefully. Eventually, it would all come together. As a child, Blankenship had been impatient with many of the activities that seemed to fascinate other children. He hated Legos and blocks. They left far too much to the imagination and he would sit, unable to visualize what to build, until the only thing he could do was throw the pieces in frustration across the room.

On the other hand, he loved putting puzzles together. That each puzzle piece had its own specific place he found soothing. There was no ambiguity involved for him. He'd had a map of the United States puzzle as a child, with each state having its own wooden piece. He could spend hours, it seemed, picking up each familiar piece, feeling its shape and eventually setting it into the frame in its proper geographical location. He could do this over and over again without getting bored, anticipating the rush of satisfaction that would come when he'd drop the final state into place and the puzzle was complete. Then he lost

Iowa, smack dab in the middle of the puzzle, and his fascination with puzzles came to an abrupt end.

He was doing now a more sophisticated version of what he'd done with the wooden USA puzzle. Instead of a wooden puzzle frame, he had a U.S. Geological Survey map. All he had to do was find each of the Moon Beach Trust deeds and see how and where they fit together.

The Moon Beach Trust deeds were clearly labeled as such and easy to identify. All the details and dates were filled in completely and, he assumed, correctly, with Simpson's bold signature affixed to each. More importantly, each deed contained a plat or map showing the dimensions of the property. Steven Castleton's prediction of the faulty work of yokels was just as inaccurate as the picture of his ex-wife as a senile old woman had been.

Blankenship found the painstaking work slow and he was not a patient man. He had to search through numerous boxes of files to find copies of the Moon Beach Trust deeds and their accompanying plats. His throat burned from the dust and his muscles tensed from the knowledge that he was sharing this dusty space with a host of many-legged creatures.

He was ready to give up for the day when the almost completed puzzle fell into place in front of him. When overlaid on the Geological Survey map, the Moon Beach Trust plats formed a wide, connected swath of waterfront property that covered several acres as it moved inland. The large expanse of land skirted the beach, the inlet, and conservation land to the inland side.

Except for one missing piece.

One piece was missing from the plats. Unlike the

frustration he'd felt when he lost the Iowa puzzle piece, this time the missing piece and its corresponding empty space filled him with jubilation. This missing puzzle piece might prove to be the most valuable parcel of all, right there along the shoreline and the banks of the Moon Beach Inlet.

He'd dismissed Ernestine's own home and parcel of land as small change when he'd first talked with Steven Castleton. Instead, Ernestine's little cottage and garden might just end up being his private goldmine.

Yes. Yes. That was it! That stupid Moon Beach Trust controlled most of the property Steven Castleton had hinted would be his for a song. But according to the records Blankenship found, one little piece of property didn't belong to the Trust.

In fact, from Blankenship's perspective, the property didn't belong to anyone, including Ernestine. He was unable to find any record of land ownership or property transfer. In Blankenship's mind, that meant the property was up for grabs and he intended to do just that. The fact that Ernestine's house and garden were planted directly on top of this seemingly unclaimed land was but a minor irritant and obstacle to Blankenship. As far as he was concerned, the property was already his.

Blankenship let out a sigh of contentment. He'd just found the hole in the dike. Now all he had to do was poke around that hole a bit and watch the Moon Beach community wash out in front of him.

At least, that was what he thought.

# CHAPTER THIRTY-TWO

FOR THE NEXT week, Blankenship became an uncharacteristically busy man. He researched all the Green Alliance organizations listed on the flyer to learn which were the most generously funded. From those he tried to determine the type of enterprise these organizations would be most interested in supporting financially. Whether he thought their general goals and principles were hooey was irrelevant.

By the day of the conference, Blankenship had created his own "green" persona. He had printed up a phony business prospectus, brochure, and business cards for Green Eco-Tours. While he was pissed off to learn just how much extra he had to pay for recycled paper, he figured it was part of the cost of doing business with this crowd.

Green Eco-Tours was ready to roll.

He decided he needed a focus on animals, preferably ones with cute babies. That would go a long way in an eventual media campaign and be most likely to pull in the sympathy donations. But more than a cute baby animal, he needed a well-heeled benefactor, preferably one with limited knowledge of actual nature and science. He hoped the Green Alliance would be the place where he'd find this benefactor.

He pulled into a spot between a couple of Priuses and headed toward the hotel conference center, following a crowd of aging Woodstock survivors in organic cotton. They did not give him immediate confidence that he'd find the big bucks he sought, and he knew he was treading unfamiliar water. He hoped it wouldn't be too long before he landed on solid ground.

"Good morning!" A woman wearing a Green Alliance T-shirt thrust a clipboard with a registration form in his direction. "Can I put you down for the conference and then staying for the dinner? It's gonna be an awesome day."

Blankenship grunted and pulled out his wallet. What the hell. He came to schmooze and if that meant chowing down on tofu and a bunch of plants, he figured he could do it this one time for the sake of Green Eco-Tours. He still had half a bottle of Probiotics Promise if he needed it.

The conference program filled in some of the details the flyer had outlined, but he figured he'd do best trolling around the exhibit area, eavesdropping on conversations and looking at the other participants to get a sense of who to target.

Blankenship learned only one thing in law school, but it was a talent that had served him well on more than one occasion. This was an appreciation for well-cut tailoring coupled with fine fabric. An expensive bespoke suit helped him identify very quickly a person willing and able to spend a fortune on making an impression, a person most likely to be successful in the ways he himself measured success. He realized that was why men were willing to unload a wheelbarrow full of cash on a Breitling wristwatch. Frankly he didn't care if the damn thing came from J.C. Penney or Tiffany, as long as it gave the correct time.

A good wool worsted, on the other hand, made his heart beat ever so much more appreciatively. Certainly he hadn't grown up cloaked in such elegance. Quite the contrary. Thinking about his childhood brought back the thick odor of dry cleaning solution and the whack of an industrial ironing machine as his mother starched and pressed shirts for the wealthy families in town. He remembered her apologizing to the scolding women when they complained about a scorched cuff and refused to pay, and only after they left the shop would she allow her tears to fall.

Once he'd been so angry that he ran out of the shop after a customer, yelling that she was stealing from his mother by not paying. The customer turned to stare at him before she got into her Cadillac and drove away. Her look of contempt was still able to chill him, decades later.

He pushed those thoughts out of his mind as quickly as the hiss of steam dissipated over the remembered broadcloth.

He hadn't traveled to this granola-fueled conference to relive his childhood, for crap's sake. He was moving forward with his life and he needed to concentrate his efforts on finding someone who could help him on his way. But the image of his mother toiling in that sweatshop, that disdain, only buoyed his resolve to get rich as quickly as possible no matter what it took.

Solar panels, sustainable soybean production, VOC paints, hydroponics. Blankenship drifted from display to display, feigning interest in case he would later find himself desperate enough to align with one of these endeavors.

"Good morning sir! Allow me to show you the benefits of our easy mix composter. Look at this kitchen waste." The man thrust a plastic container filled with wilted lettuce into Blankenship's face. "Now look at the black gold it will become in just a few short weeks with the Magic Mix Self-Composter." He held up another container filled with dark brown compost. "What do you think of that?"

It was too much for Blankenship.

"What do I think? I think it looks like dog shit, not black gold."

So far, the fair was not working out as Blankenship had hoped. A small crowd of people was gathering around them and he realized he'd have been better off just dumping the compost on the front of the guy's Magic Mix display and keeping his mouth shut.

One of the bystanders spoke up and broke the tension. "Hey man! I love this thing. Let me see how it works."

Magic Mix man looked grateful. He began gushing about the ease of composting with his contraption to a small group of people who seemed genuinely interested in it. Blankenship drifted away unnoticed.

He knew he needed to be less confrontational. This was difficult for him. He nodded indiscriminately as he passed from table to table and people tried to convince him, and whoever else passed by, that their green initiative was the next great thing to save the planet.

He kept his mouth shut after the Magic Mix incident. He wasn't listening so much as looking around, hoping that he'd be able to see at a glance his new partner.

Bingo. She was wearing a tailored suit, Valentino perhaps, and he longed to rub his fingers against its exquisite soft fabric. Her scent was subtle and interesting enough that Blankenship assumed it, too, to be extremely expensive.

She was standing somewhat aloof from the crowd and Blankenship hoped she was looking for the same thing he was: a cause.

He decided to scope her out from a distance, listen to her talk, see what vendors interested her before he'd bait his line and start fishing. He followed her as she walked from kiosk to kiosk without speaking to anyone.

Tears formed in her eyes as she watched a video of baby egrets trapped in a greasy spill.

"Beautiful animals," Blankenship murmured in what he hoped was a sympathetic tone. "It's tragic to see what's happening to them." For all he knew or cared, the birds could be swimming happily in a pool of cabernet sauvignon, not feather clogging oil.

She looked at him through her tears and nodded. "I just want to be able to do something to help."

For a moment, Blankenship's heart stood still. He felt like he had just been given the keys to a glorious kingdom. All he had to do was open the door and ask her to step across the threshold.

# CHAPTER THIRTY-THREE

"WHY DON'T WE get something to drink and go some place quiet so we can talk? I might have an idea that would interest you." Blankenship tried his best at a winning smile.

Sonofabitch. Some asshole bumped into him and he dropped his brochures, just when he was trying to be his most debonair best. He swooped them up and motioned to the French doors leading out to a patio. Blankenship grazed the woman's arm ever so lightly but, he hoped, with authority, to help steer her toward the wrought iron settee framed by heavy wisteria branches. The fabric felt as rich as it looked and Blankenship inhaled softly with pleasure.

"I'm Vaughn Blankenship. Attorney Vaughn Blankenship." Blankenship held out his hand formally, and held hers for a fraction of a second too long after shaking it. "I'm very glad to meet you." This was the first honest thing he'd said in days.

Her hands were long and slender, her handshake firm. "Celeste Armstrong. What is this idea that you think would interest me?" Blankenship couldn't tell if her smile had an undertone of sarcasm and he stammered briefly.

But as he visualized Ernestine's coastline and tidal creek running up into the wetlands rich with wildlife like whatever the hell kind of bird made Celeste go teary-eyed, he realized just how much he wanted that property, or at least what he thought that property could do for him. His pulse quickened as he described the coastline and the water with more animation than he'd even dreamed was possible.

"Here's what I want to do. I want to share this spectacular setting with a special kind of ecotourist. One who can appreciate this completely natural setting and travel through the wetlands quietly, unobtrusively, by kayak or canoe. A very special kind of ecotourist, one whose busy professional and civic pursuits might not allow the time for travel by conventional means to get to an out of the way treasure such as the setting Green Eco-Tours provides." He gushed on about the special ecotourist before switching gears to gush about the vast number of species found only in this area, which he was now calling Tidewater Crossing.

He talked about exclusivity and how only a select few serious ecotourists, the kind with real money, would be able to take part in this adventure, to have the privilege of becoming part-owners in this wilderness sanctuary. This exclusivity would support the scientific research efforts that Tidewater Crossing and Green Eco-Tours intended to conduct.

Celeste listened intently, particularly to the notion of exclusivity.

Blankenship went on: "Only a select tier of people will

be able to qualify, if you will, for membership." He put air quotes around 'qualify' as he spoke. "This elite cadre of supporters will pay to see the wilderness as few others have seen it. And their contributions in return will actually support reclamation efforts where needed. God knows there's more than enough damage to go around. I see it as a win-win situation for everyone, both the ecotourists and the environment." He racked his brain trying to remember what animal had made Celeste cry. It would have been nice to mention the poor creature here.

Blankenship also neglected to mention the linchpin of the entire endeavor and what would allow rich people with too much money and not enough time or real interest to visit Tidewater Crossing and check something else off their bucket lists.

That would be the helicopter pad that Blankenship envisioned, poured directly on the site where Ernestine's cottage currently stood. This is what would allow his "exclusive ecotourism" model to work, as tourists could be rushed in from the expensive resorts stacked miles away along the coast, far from the serenity of undeveloped Moon Beach. Once the helicopter landed, the exclusive tourists could be loaded onto kayaks or canoes and schlepped upstream to see any remaining wildlife that hadn't high-tailed it out when the first noisy helicopter landed on the dunes.

By the time serious investors found out about the helipad, it would be too late. They would have already invested their money and Blankenship would, he hoped, be settling into a South American paradise to live off whatever he'd managed to steal from them. Ernestine and the Moon Beach locals could keep the rest of the damn properties. As if they'd be worth anything with a stinking helipad smack in the middle of the wetlands.

Actually, Blankenship didn't much care if the helipad ever got built. He had some vague notion it would probably be illegal to build a structure like that so close to the coast, but he intended to assure potential investors from the business side that he had obtained the necessary permits since an essential part of his bogus plan and its cachet was its development as a scientific research site.

All he wanted was the investors' money safely hidden in a bank account in the Caymans so he could draw on it from his hacienda in the southern hemisphere. He'd already signed up for Spanish lessons.

"What will your organization be doing to help the egrets and other animals already damaged by our recent oil spills?" Celeste's question brought him back to the present.

"Ah, an excellent question. I can tell you are a true nature lover." Blankenship stalled as he tried to make up an appropriate answer. "We will be working with a team of biologists from the State University as well as a couple of people in the oil industry who will look at the damage in our specific area and come up with ways to mitigate what's already been done. Of course, we will run a rehabilitation clinic for any animals that have been injured by past environmental mistakes." He was so pleased with his on the fly answer that he thought about revising some of his promotional materials to include these new elements.

Celeste had heard enough to open her checkbook when Blankenship said these magic words: "We can make you a Founding Patron with the right donation."

She smiled at him. "How much?"

Blankenship could hardly believe his good luck. Celeste Armstrong seemed genuinely interested in his proposal, particularly with its new addition. More importantly, she appeared to be loaded. She didn't flinch when he told her how much becoming a Founding Patron would set her back. When her eyes welled up again with tears over the plight of the baby whatevers, he had a quick pang of what could conceivably develop into ethical remorse, but he stifled it. The financial support she could bring to Green Eco-Tours and Tidewater Crossing and, more importantly, to his new life, pushed ethics into the same black hole as Ernestine's property and the fate of the wildlife in and around Moon Beach.

He realized that he might be able to bilk Ms. Armstrong out of more than just a substantial financial contribution to Green Eco-Tours if he were able to turn on his own personal charm.

He was well aware that charm was not one of his strong suits, but greed and his desire for an early retirement pushed him into a new sphere of interaction at the personal level.

"May I call you Celeste?" He smiled and with this one small step entered an entirely new realm of deception.

# CHAPTER THIRTY-FOUR

LIZZIE STUMBLED ALONG the sand, barely able to see over the tears that filled her eyes and streamed down her cheeks. She scooped up a handful of shells and tossed them into the lick of seafoam that washed up and covered her toes. She tossed another, and then another.

Damn. She'd have to scoop up the whole beach to fill the emptiness she felt inside. That was the essence of her life: a random assortment of flotsam and jetsam she threw around as haphazardly as she tossed the shells. And everything washed away with the tide.

"You'll never be able to change the shoreline that way, my dear." A soft voice crept up behind her.

Lizzie whirled around. "Ernestine! You scared me."

"That's the thing about walking on the sand. It's easy to come up behind someone when they think they're alone. But you're rarely all alone, at least not here. There's always someone or something that's got your back."

Ernestine looked at Lizzie's blotchy face. "You look like you might maybe want to set a spell. Care to join me?"

"That would be terrific." Lizzie wiped her nose on the

hem of her shirt and tried to smile.

"Come on, then." Ernestine turned and started walking. Lizzie followed, struggling to keep up with Ernestine's pace.

Ernestine's little cottage was the same turquoise as her eyes, and bright pink shutters flanked its windows. A wild tangle of pink and purple flowers edged the porch and the uneven flagstones that led from the dune path into her yard. In contrast, neat rows of vegetables lined up in the garden at the far corner of the yard. A scarecrow in a faded Grateful Dead T-shirt presided over the orderly collards, tomatoes, and herbs.

Ernestine held open the door and Lizzie walked into the cool space, fragrant with the spicy scent of a dozen orchid plants in the bay window alcove.

"Oh! Thank you. I feel better already."

"Sometimes it's nice to have a little company. I'm glad I ran into you, too." Ernestine moved around her kitchen and set two jelly glasses down on the table.

She smiled at Lizzie. "I think this might call for something a little special." She pulled a half-gallon jug out of a cabinet and poured two inches of honey colored liquid into each glass.

She pushed a glass toward Lizzie. "Let me know what you think. Better go slow."

Lizzie took a tentative sip. Her mouth and throat burned for an instant, then she was left with a faint taste of peach as the liquid slid toward her stomach. "Whoa." She looked at Ernestine. "This stuff is lethal. Is it moonshine?"

Ernestine laughed. "Nah. But it might as well be, for the wallop it packs. It's an old-timey recipe from my grand-daddy. I like to keep some on hand to keep the chill out, especially that bone chill that comes from somethin' other than the temperature, if you know what I mean."

Despite the warm weather, Lizzie hadn't realized until Ernestine spoke just how cold she felt inside. She grabbed a paper napkin and blew her nose. "It's pretty powerful stuff."

Ernestine had been right, as usual. Warmth seeped through Lizzie's body and she began to relax. The two women sat there in silence until their glasses were empty.

Ernestine focused her blue eyes on Lizzie as she watched her fold and unfold her rumpled napkin repeatedly. "You gonna wear that poor thing out if you keep worrying it like that." Lizzie stopped and looked at Ernestine.

"I…" Lizzie's voice trailed off, then started again. "I feel kind of lost. Like I'm all scattered and running around in a thousand different directions. Like my head is cut up into separate little compartments and nothing fits together."

She slumped in her chair. "Look at people like Anne, and you and Vince. You get stuff done. Even though I know you've had tons of crap to deal with.

"I'm like that stuff I was scooping up on the beach. A bunch of shells and seaweed and an occasional seagull feather. None of it fits together. But it doesn't really matter because the tide'll just wash it away and start all over again with new junk."

Ernestine picked up the jug and poured just enough to cover the bottom of each glass. Lizzie held her glass with both hands and rocked it back and forth, staring at the motion of the liquid.

"I'm a mess. And there's, ah, some other stuff, too."

Lizzie pushed the image of a tall, dark figure and angry voices from her mind.

"I can't focus on getting back to work. I used to be good at putting funky stuff together. It's what I do. Or what I did.

"Now I can't do anything. I act like a jerk—" she stopped mid-sentence. "And I'm afraid to let anyone get too close in case they find out just what an idiot I am." She blew her nose in the tattered napkin and tossed it in the wastebasket.

Ernestine paused before responding. "No one thinks you're an idiot, Lizzie. Confused about life, maybe. And still dealing with your mother's death. That's not easy for anyone, especially someone as young as you. You need to give yourself some time to heal.

"Moon Beach is some kind of good medicine for just about everyone. Go easy on yourself. Get back to doing what you're good at, even if you have to fake it for a while. You can put things together again—even your funky stuff, whatever that is.

"You'll see." Ernestine focused her steely eyes directly on Lizzie. "Trust me on this."

# CHAPTER THIRTY-FIVE

LIZZIE STUDIED THE table filled with recycled paper pamphlets printed with soy-based inks. She hoped Ernestine was right and the twenty bucks she'd just spent on the conference registration wouldn't turn out to be a waste. She stuffed a couple of flyers half-heartedly into her notebook, but so far, the Green Alliance Fair seemed like a total bust for her. She had talked to any number of earnest and enthusiastic people at the various booths, but nothing was clicking for her.

"You look lost." The long-haired man in the Green Alliance T-shirt smiled at her. "Can I help you find something?"

"Umm, I hope so." Lizzie looked at the man. "I'm interested in seeing if there're any metal recycling or scrap yards with booths here."

"You're kidding, right?" The man looked confused, maybe slightly amused.

Lizzie sighed. She'd sat frozen in the parking lot for a good fifteen minutes before finally deciding to take a chance and go into the fair. She didn't feel like explaining herself and her life. She was waiting for him to make some stupid comment about what's a pretty girl like you doing looking for a junk yard. Fortunately, he kept his mouth shut as she stared at him.

"No, I'm not kidding." Her voice shook and she knew she was too loud. "I'm trying to find a decent salvage or scrap yard. Recycling. You've heard of it? It's kind of a green thing."

He looked surprised at the energy in her voice. "Yeah, of course. I just assumed—most of the organizations here are dealing with, uh, natural stuff. Like ecology. Birds. Animals. Not scrap metal. I don't think this is the right place for you." He turned abruptly and walked away from her.

Lizzie bit her tongue and stuffed the photographs back in her notebook, glad she hadn't blown her time and what little self-confidence she felt by showing them to him.

What a jerk. She hated it when people became so self-righteous about their beliefs they couldn't look outside their own little boxes to see the world from a different perspective. This guy might want to save the earth, but he certainly could benefit from being a little more down to earth.

Maybe she'd just spent too much time in Moon Beach with folks like Ernestine and Vince, the most down to earth people she knew.

Vince. She imagined him walking around the Green Alliance Fair dressed in the chicken suit. That would wake up the crowd. The thought made her giggle and she felt better than she had since pulling into the parking lot. So far, everyone she'd talked to seemed so serious and it was rubbing off on her.

Maybe one of these days she'd show Vince and Ernestine some of the pictures and see what they thought. She'd kept them to herself since arriving in Moon Beach, knowing they'd be sure to spark a confrontation with her dad. He'd had such strong feelings about that part of her life and he'd tried to steer her in a different direction. Unfortunately, her father had been right. If only she'd listened to him instead of digging in her heels!

Her mind swung back to the present and the Green Alliance Fair when she saw a familiar face near the refreshment table. Wasn't it that obnoxious Blankenship? The one who'd been trying to steal Ernestine's property? What the hell was a jerk like him doing here? Despite her bad encounter with the Green Alliance guy over the scrap metal, most of the folks she'd talked to so far seemed to have a genuine desire to do some good in the world.

Blankenship, on the other hand, seemed to her like nothing more than a gold digger who'd just as happily stir fry endangered animals as save them. He was so deep in conversation with a woman that Lizzie thought she could sneak in behind him and eavesdrop without his noticing. And get something to drink while she was at it.

A young man bounded up as she sidled over to the gallon jugs of cold-pressed organic cider.

"Hey! Aren't you the—"

Lizzie shook her head no and tried to walk away from her new admirer. But he was insistent: "Didn't I see you on—"

Lizzie shook her head again, but the man came closer. She backed up to get away from him and jostled Blankenship's arm just as he was pulling some papers out of his briefcase.

"Son of a bitch!" he said under his breath as the papers fell to the floor.

"Sorry!" Lizzie kept her face down as she picked up the scattered papers, hoping he wouldn't recognize her. She stuffed some of them into her notebook and handed the rest to Blankenship as she walked away. Right now she needed a breather more than she needed a drink.

He was intent on his conversation and never once looked at the woman who picked up the papers he'd dropped. Never seemed to notice what was missing. Of course he hadn't bothered to thank her. Hadn't they been through this once before?

Lizzie paused when she got to the outside door. She was thirsty and, damn it, she'd paid for the conference. That included the food. She turned to go back and get a cup of cider. Blankenship was bound to have moved on by then.

As she poured a cup, she could see the young man who'd been following her earlier heading toward her. Screw it, she was going to get her cider and go outside and drink it in peace.

"Can I at least have your autograph?" He pulled out his conference program. Lizzie burst out laughing. It was better than clobbering him, which she also considered doing.

"I don't know who you think I am, but you're wrong. I'm nobody."

He looked puzzled. "You're not on TV?"

"Totally not. I don't even watch the stuff."

He grinned at her and put his conference program back in his pocket. "Bet you think I'm an idiot. I thought you were on *Idol*." Lizzie grinned back. He seemed a bit more likable than he'd been a minute earlier, reminding her of a hyperactive puppy. It was a relief to see someone here at the fair who didn't seem so serious.

"So how come you're here? My roommate hyped this thing as some great opportunity to learn about everything natural and tree-huggy. I came because I'm interested in new ways of making tofu, but there's not much here for me. Tofu making is sort of a lost art and I guess tofu makers are lost artists." He laughed. "But I'd rather be found. How about you?"

Lizzie breathed deeply and thought, why not? At the worst, he'd laugh at her, and he'd already laughed at himself.

"I'm interested in junk art. Made out of the stuff most people throw away. I thought maybe there would be something, someone here who would be into that." Lizzie pulled a couple of the pictures out of her notebook. "Stuff like this."

He was silent for a minute while studying the pictures, then he whistled. "Wow. You made these?"

"Yeah. These are some old pieces."

"Well, you should get working on some new pieces. These are amazing."

"Thanks. Maybe I will one of these days."

"Nah, not one of these days. You should be doing it right now."

"Maybe." Lizzie shrugged. "It's complicated."

"Isn't everything? I mean, even making tofu is. You gotta get things just right or else everything blows up." He held out his hand. "I'm Todd, Todd the tofu guy. Pleased to meet you."

"Lizzie here."

"Um, Lizzie, it's none of my business, but you know that guy you bumped into back there? I'd steer clear of him if I were you. The guy just smells like trouble."

"I'll keep that in mind."

"You sure you haven't been on *Idol*?" He winked at her. "Y'know, I don't even have a TV. Wouldn't watch the stuff unless you paid me, and believe me, nobody is. Wouldn't know an idol from a schmidol. But sometimes that's the only way I can get people to talk to me."

Lizzie groaned and made a face at him.

"Hey, it worked, didn't it? You're talking to me. I swear, making stuff up works better than telling the truth some of the time."

"I'll keep that in mind, Todd."

"Hey, and Lizzie?"

She turned to look at him. "Yeah?"

"You're wrong. Ain't no way you're nobody. Now take care." He winked at her again and waved as he walked away.

She just wished she agreed with him.

# CHAPTER THIRTY-SIX

PETER COOPER STOOD nervously at the front of the Friends of the Wild booth. The Green Alliance Fair was his first opportunity to run the booth, and he hoped to not only make a good impression, but to totally knock the socks off the rest of the team with the number of "Friends" or even "Patrons" of the Wild he'd been able to sign up.

So far, five people had donated fifteen bucks each. Not bad, but certainly not what he'd been hoping for. He'd been hoping for a boatload of contributions so he could actually get to that hands-on experience he'd been promised during his phone interview back home in South Dakota.

Getting this internship had been a triumph for him. He wanted to see the world, or at least the country, and the opportunity to work for less than minimum wage during school break with the promise of a great line on his resume if and when he graduated from college seemed, at the time, terrific.

Once he'd ridden a series of buses down from Rapid City, South Dakota, though, he wasn't so sure. It seemed like his entire internship was wrapped around trying to get people to give money to Friends of the Wild. Money was important, of course, for an organization as well as an individual trying to survive. He realized that once he saw how small his paycheck was. At least the Friends had steered him to decent low-cost housing with other young workers. Otherwise he knew he'd be back on a Greyhound bus heading home before his next rent payment was due.

His bigger disappointment, though, was with Friends of the Wild itself. He'd been led to believe he would actually be working outdoors, where he could interact with the ecosystem and flora and fauna of the southern coastal region he longed to see.

He'd spent the best times of his young life in a kayak exploring the lakes and rivers around the Black Hills, and he wanted to do the same along the nearby saltwater estuaries. The prospect of writing a senior honors thesis comparing the different ecosystems he could explore via kayak had crossed his mind more than once, and when he closed his eyes, he saw himself winning the prestigious University Research Medal for the work he had yet to begin.

He'd shared that dream only with his grandmother back home. She'd been so thrilled and proud she even gave him the money for his bus ticket south. Paying it forward, she called it. He smiled when he thought how excited Gram had been for him, how happy to help him reach for his dream.

But so far, his internship had consisted of making phone calls or going door to door in hopes of gathering financial support. He'd yet to step foot in salt water as a Friend of the Wild.

That had to change. He couldn't bear to disappoint Gram or himself any longer. The Green Alliance Fair was showing him there were other nature oriented organizations in the area; perhaps one of them would offer him a more hands-on experience than Friends of the Wild. It wouldn't hurt him to look around and explore his options. If he had been ambitious enough to travel this far south on his own, surely he had the wherewithal to find and grab onto a different, better opportunity now that he was here on the coast.

So he viewed each of the people who wandered past Friends of the Wild from two lenses: one looking for a major contribution to the Friends–and the resulting uptick in his own personal value to the organization–and one that looked out first and foremost for Peter Cooper's own interests.

"Hi there." Peter used his big smile on the next person to approach the booth. "Let me tell you a little bit about Friends of the Wild." The woman seemed startled when he jumped out in front of her. But she looked rich, certainly richer than most of the people who had shuffled past his booth. She smelled like flowers and for an instant Peter saw the vast fields of purple and gold wildflowers he knew from childhood. He felt a swift pang of homesickness.

"We're interested in preserving our coastal environment and are looking for your help." He recited the Friends of the Wild sales pitch and smiled, making eye contact since she seemed vaguely interested in what he was saying.

"People like you have the power to save our most

threatened species and to save these species right now with your generous donations." He didn't want to beg, but he was aware of the rising pitch of his voice as he spoke. He stopped to breathe in deeply and, he hoped, to give her time to think about how much her money could help these poor endangered plants and animals. Not to mention Peter Cooper's own sales statistics.

"I certainly want to help in any way I can. Will a hundred dollars suffice?"

Yes! He exhaled as she took out her checkbook. He had just signed up his first Friends of the Wild Century Sponsor.

"Thank you, ma'am. I'm sure you'll find being a very special Friend of the Wild is well worth your generous contribution. You make our work possible and the animals thank you."

As soon as he said it, he realized he had no idea if any animals were actually being protected by Friends of the Wild. The notion of a bunch of alligators and herons joining together in a chorus of gratitude was patently ridiculous and his dream of a dynamite senior honors thesis seemed as distant to him as the coastal ecology he'd not yet had the opportunity to explore as a Friends of the Wild intern.

By mid-afternoon, Peter was getting discouraged. He'd brought in a decent amount of small donor contributions for the Friends of the Wild, and that hundred bucks from the Century Sponsor with the nice perfume certainly helped a lot.

But he'd yet to make the connection he hoped for, the connection that would turn his relationship with the beautiful coastal region from a distant observer and salesman into a researcher who could actually make a positive contribution to the area's natural resource development.

Then Peter's luck changed. Vaughn Blankenship and Green Eco-Tours walked into his life.

"Sir, can I tell you a little about Friends of the Wild and what we are doing here in the coastal area?"

The man in the dark gray business suit looked at the young man and nodded.

Peter started right in. "We are interested in preserving the unique flora and fauna of the area, particularly those species that, if not actually endangered yet, are on a watch list because their numbers are low and their survival is considered fragile." These words were taken directly from the Friends of the Wild promotional material and Peter recited them as he had so many times before.

The man appeared to be listening intently to him. Peter noticed his name tag read "Green Eco-Tours." As Gram used to tell him, opportunity may knock, but you've got to open the door and let it in.

Peter took a deep breath and started to veer down a new path, promoting himself rather than Friends of the Wild.

"Actually, sir, I am looking for an opportunity to get even more involved in saving these endangered species. And I'd like to share my, ah, considerable knowledge about ecology with others, perhaps as a tour guide."

The man smiled at him and stuck out his hand. "Enough with the 'sir' already. I'm Vaughn Blankenship. Tell me more about what you'd like to do." Blankenship squinted at Peter's name tag. "Peter, is it?"

Peter nodded and breathed a sigh of relief. "Thank you,

sir. I mean, Mr. Blankenship. These coastal waters are perfect for touring from a kayak." He hoped Green Eco-Tours used kayaks. "I'd love to take folks on tours and use my scientific background to talk about the local environment." He thought he saw more than a flicker of interest in Blankenship's face and decided to stretch his scientific background and experience a bit.

"My current university research involves studying the balance between aquatic species as development encroaches on the environment. And I'm comparing the impact in salt and fresh water environments. I've already collected a lot of data." He was startled by how easily stretching the truth came to him.

Blankenship smiled at him. "Fascinating. You seem so young to be doing such important work."

Now Peter was worried. Perhaps he'd laid it on too thick. But he was desperate and Green Eco-Tours was right in front of him. "I'm just really interested in this work. And getting outdoors to do it. I'll do anything to make that happen."

"I hope so. I might be able to offer you something that will, ah, work out well for both of us." Blankenship smiled again.

Peter snapped the panels of the Friends of the Wild display shut at the end of the Green Alliance Fair. It had been a long day, but he felt an exhilaration that he had, finally, made the contact he needed to explore this beautiful coastal region.

There were some troubling contradictions and holes in the Green Eco-Tours model that Peter was willing to overlook, given Blankenship's promise: he, Peter Cooper, would actually be leading tours into the tidal reaches that Green Eco-Tours owned, or would own soon enough. He, Peter Cooper, would be Green Eco-Tours' scientific expert.

Between his experience with Friends of the Wild and his new collaboration with Green Eco-Tours, Peter envisioned his senior honors thesis as already written. When he closed his eyes, he could hear the applause as he accepted the University Research Medal.

He could hardly wait to get started. He sent a quick email to Gram to let her know he was finally on his way.

# CHAPTER THIRTY-SEVEN

ERNESTINE SENSED THEIR presence in her garden before she heard them talking. She set her cup of coffee down and headed outside.

"What the hell do you think you're doing?" She didn't need to ask; it was obvious. Two men, one beefy and the other skinny as a rail, were sticking survey pegs directly into her neat rows of collards.

The third man, wearing a hard hat and lounging against the side of the pickup truck, looked at her. He must be the boss, she thought, though why anyone would need a hard hat to supervise guys running a survey instrument through a person's backyard was beyond her.

"Surveying." He spat into her petunias and she just barely resisted swinging her walking stick into his shiny hat.

"Surveying? Whatever for?"

"The new owner."

"What the hell are you talking about? This is my property."

He shrugged. "Beats me. Me and my crew just do what

we get paid to do. Don't really care who owns what, just so long's we get our money, you know what I'm saying?" He was getting ready to thwack out another loogie when he saw Ernestine's face and her raised walking stick. He swallowed instead. "Hope it ain't a problem for you."

"If you leave before I call the police it won't be a problem." Ernestine's hands were shaking.

"Ma'am, no need to bother." The heavyset man spoke as he and the thin man walked out of the garden and back toward the truck. "We done and heading out now anyways. I hope we din't disturb you too much. Have a blessed day." When the men got into the truck, excited barking came from the rear of the cab as three furry heads bobbed up and down to greet them.

The truck headed off before Ernestine could find out who the men worked for. She figured it had to be Blankenship or one of his cronies, and when the legal envelope arrived in the mail the next day, she had her answer.


Bernie studied the creamy legal papers in his hand and then set them on his desk. He rubbed his hand slowly across his forehead before looking at Ernestine.

"You're right. There is a problem with your property. Or at least there could be, if Blankenship digs in his heels."

Ernestine ground her cigarillo into the ashtray. "What do you mean? It's my damn property."

"According to this, it's not." Bernie waved a sheet of paper in front of him "He claims there's no title on record for your property. Why not?"

"You don't understand what it was like back then. Two

151

category four hurricanes in a row wiped out just about everything here in Moon Beach and pretty far inland as well. There were no county offices left, and even if there had been, the road was washed out for months. Nobody was thinking about stinking titles.

"Don't look at me like that." Ernestine scowled at Bernie. "You weren't here. You can't judge me or anyone else for what we did just to survive."

Ernestine was right. It was far too easy to judge another person without knowing the full extent of the circumstances in their lives. Bernie thought back to an earlier time in his own life. Too bad stepping into another's skin for a while hadn't been the first tenet of law school.

Come to think of it, the ability to walk a mile in someone else's shoes made good sense in just about every endeavor, even though Bernie seriously doubted that it made the curriculum in business school any more than it had shown up in any ethics class during his law school years. The overriding principle always seemed to be to come out ahead of everyone else no matter what. If that involved grabbing someone else's shoes so you could walk across the hot coals while they fried their feet, so what. That was the American way.

Ernestine's voice brought him back to the present. "I told you, we had the two storms back to back and everything fell apart. There were no roads, no food, no water. Nothing.

"Elrod Wilson was desperate to get his family inland and closer to whatever we tried to call civilization that year. Poor man had all those kids and that wife who'd just about given up on life. He was too damn proud to take what he called charity. So I bought the place from him."

Ernestine sniffed. Her hands were shaking as she reached for her cigarillos. "People were dirt poor. And there wasn't even any dirt! We didn't even have roofs over our heads or clean drinking water for months. It's only because of shoreline accretion and all that crazy dredging activity up at the port that there's anything solid there right now. It was underwater back then."

Bernie sighed. "I get it. Everyone did the best they could at the time. But we need to go head to head with Blankenship now over your property."

"Why? It's my land and I have no intention of giving it up. This just compensation he's offering is a joke. A bad joke. And even less than what Steven was willing to pay me for it. Where's he come off with all that shit?"

"He claims because there's not a registered deed, it's unclaimed property and the state or some conservation group like his can take it over. It would become a public trust for stewardship of the land."

"That's bullshit," Ernestine said. "Isn't it?"

Bernie sighed again. "Pretty much, but we'll still have to jump through some hoops to prove it's bullshit. I don't know what Blankenship has up his sleeve with this Green Eco-Tours, but I'll bet it's not saving the planet. As far as I can tell, the only thing green in his eyes is money.

"The biggest problem, though, may not even be Blankenship himself, but his partners. I don't know much about Friends of the Wild, but I do know that many of the conservation groups out there are not what they appear to be. They may have started out with good intentions, but over time they turned into fronts for land-hungry conglomerates."

"I don't get what the big guys have to do with it," Ernestine said.

"The big guys have big pockets. If one or more of their corporate partners discover our bit of paradise, they might try to influence our esteemed state legislators to make your so-called unclaimed land public property. Take over your property by eminent domain and suck up the rest of Moon Beach under the guise of environmental stewardship. Unfortunately, the lure of cash will always sway some of our elected officials.

"Before any of that happens, we need to convince Blankenship to move on. That Moon Beach is the last place in the world he wants for his little project. But we better move fast, before he gets some of these partners interested in your backyard. A registered deed with clear title would speed things up. Time is of the essence and all that."

"You don't get it, Bernie. Back then you'd find a place you could scratch into at high tide and put a shack up on it, call it home. Nobody thought about owning the damn swamp. A deed, my ass."

With that, Ernestine walked out the door, slamming it as she went.

# CHAPTER THIRTY-EIGHT

"THAT WAS WEIRD," Lizzie said.

"What was?" Vince walked down the driveway toward her.

"Ernestine. She came down the stairs from Bernie and Anne's looking like a ghost. I waved at her and she just nodded. Look at her. She's already halfway down the beach walkway."

Lizzie started toward the walkway and Vince touched her arm to stop her.

"Leave her be. Looks like she doesn't want company right now."

Lizzie shrugged. "You're probably right, but I wonder what's going on."

They both looked up when they heard Bernie's flip-flops clattering down the steps toward them.

"What's going on with E?" Lizzie asked.

Bernie shook his head. "Bad news. That Blankenship idiot is still trying to nab her property. Turns out Ernestine never registered a deed or title to her own property and he's going after it on the grounds that it's public property."

Vince frowned and looked at Bernie. "Ernestine's not going to get kicked out of her own home, is she?"

"Not if I have anything to do with it. But it's going to take some time and effort. I'm going to start nosing around to see what skeletons Blankenship keeps in his closet. I'll bet it's full of them. Should be able to use that info to, ah, convince him to move Green Eco-Tours somewhere other than Moon Beach. I suspect he hasn't filed all the appropriate paperwork himself for this venture. I intend to nail him if that's the case. If Blankenship's already started legal proceedings to get her land, I'll file an appeal today. That should slow him down."

"Is there anything we can do?"

"Let me handle the legal issues. I'm actually looking forward to jousting with the guy. But some, ah, creative strategies to persuade him to just drop the whole project and leave Moon Beach alone might be in order."

He smiled at them both. "I certainly won't stand in the way of anyone who wants to give that a shot. Especially if I don't know about it. Now, if you'll excuse me, I think we all have some work to do." Bernie headed back up the steps.

Vince and Lizzie watched as Bernie disappeared into his house.

"You in?" Vince looked at Lizzie sideways.

"Of course. Any ideas?"

"Not a clue. At least, not yet."

"Me neither," Lizzie said.

"But I want to slam that bastard for trying to screw Ernestine."

"Vince? Let's try to scare him some while we do this, okay? I wouldn't mind seeing him sweat a little."

"Fine with me. I'm willing to do just about anything for Ernestine. As long as we can get Blankenship out of the picture for good."

The thought of saving Ernestine while handing Blankenship his just desserts brought a smile to Vince's face.

The notion of doing so alongside Lizzie warmed his entire spirit.

Bernie picked up the phone and entered a number. "Spence? Long time no talk." He squeezed a smiley-faced sponge ball as he settled into the call. "Listen, I need the scoop on a guy named Vaughn Blankenship, probably not his real name. Says he's an attorney. Seems to know something about state law, so I'd start looking for him in state. Guy must be in his forties. I'll send you a picture from a party he crashed at my wife's bookstore not long ago. He's the dour-looking guy standing next to Anne. See what you can find."

Bernie had successfully defended Spence on an extortion charge a decade ago. The six months Spence spent in prison as a potential flight risk during the trial had provided a valuable networking opportunity. Spence had contacts, resources, and techniques that enabled him to ferret out information with breathtaking speed. Bernie provided legal counsel whenever Spence needed it. The relationship worked well for both of them.

Bernie hung up and started his own inquiry into the legal status of Blankenship's enterprises.

# CHAPTER THIRTY-NINE

"SO, ERNESTINE, TELL me something about how you got your property." Lizzie settled into the little kitchen with a cup of Ernestine's super-strength coffee.

"That was so long ago. Elrod Wilson and his family lived in a little shack right about where my oleanders stand now. He'd cobbled it together out of old plywood, corrugated tin, spit, whatever he could scrounge. Those storms came and scattered pieces of it all along the coast.

"Poor Elrod was desperate, but too proud to take a loan we both knew he'd never be able to repay. So I said I'd buy his land."

"Did you get a deed or any paper from him?"

"Sweet Jesus, Lizzie. You're beginning to sound just like Bernie." Ernestine sniffed and looked out the window.

"Wait a second. You said he was too proud for a handout. Didn't he give you something for the money, just to save face or something?"

Ernestine nodded and stood up. "Just this." She walked into her living room and stretched to pull a heavy black volume from the top of a bookcase. When she opened the

Bible, several loose pages fell to the floor. Lizzie picked them up as Ernestine shuffled through the book.

She handed Lizzie a single yellowed sheet of lined paper. "I filed it in Genesis. Figured both them floods amounted to something." Her laugh sounded hollow. "That's all I got."

Lizzie looked at the paper, brittle with age. "Can I borrow this for a couple of days?"

"You can keep the damn thing for all I care," Ernestine said. "Look at it. Elrod could barely write and it's not even clear what he was selling."

Lizzie examined the paper more carefully. It wasn't much, but it would have to do.

"I might be able to help out," she said.

# CHAPTER FORTY

THE LARGE FIGURE filled the entire doorway to Ernestine's cottage.

She scowled at him. "Weren't you here with that dickwad?"

"Ma'am?"

"I've seen you before." She stared at the tattoo on the man's arm. "You surveyed my property for that bastard Blankenship."

"Yes ma'am. That's why I'm back." He frowned and paused, as if figuring out what to say next.

"Well? I haven't got all day."

"Here." He thrust a small burlap bag at Ernestine. "Uh, the missus, she real good at potions and what not. I told her that man was fixing to do you bad and she got busy." He shifted from one foot to the other. "You got anything he put his hands on?"

"Blankenship? I've got all these blasted letters he keeps sending me."

"That ought to do. She say you don't need much, so maybe tear off a corner of a page or something."

"Then what?" Ernestine took the bag from him.

"She say you mix this," he pointed to the little bag, "with a little sea water under the full moon. Dig a hole somewhere on your land, put the paper or whatever in the hole. Pour the water on top of that." He mimicked pouring a cup of water with his right hand. "You gotta talk to that man while you working, tell him leave you be. Then you put your dirt back on top. And wait for it to take."

"She any good?"

"Well, a lot of folks swear by her."

"Do you?"

"Yes ma'am. She say the day she first met me she went right home and mixed up a love potion." He grinned. "That was twenty-two years ago and it ain't wore off yet."

Ernestine looked at him with interest. "It might be worth a try. I haven't got anything else."

The man nodded. "Could be enough to scare that fellow off. You could use some help, if you don't mind me saying."

"I guess it can't do any harm. Thank you." Ernestine reached out her hand and it got lost in his big handshake.

"Hope it works. Have a blessed day now." He turned, climbed into his red pickup truck and drove off.

The crisp rows of Ernestine's vegetable garden shone clearly in the moonlight when she opened the door and walked into her yard. She held a small burlap bag and her walking stick in her left hand and carried an earthenware cup in her right hand. She walked slowly all around the property and finally headed over the dunes to the water's edge. She knelt down in the sand and lowered the cup, carefully scooping it into the water to fill it.

Once back in the yard, she walked slowly around the property again before kneeling near the oleander bushes. She pulled an ornate silver spoon from her pocket and began digging a hole in the sandy soil. When she was satisfied, she tore up a rumpled piece of paper and dropped it in the hole. She opened the burlap bag and released its spicy aroma. Then she carefully mixed the contents of the bag into the earthenware cup. She poured the potion into the hole.

"Blankenship, be gone. Leave this beautiful place as it is. Find another way to feed your greed. Or it will all come back on you," she said softly. Then her voice changed and she began chanting. Something musical, something other than words tumbled out of her mouth. When she was finished, she patted dirt and sand back into the hole and smoothed over the surface before rising again. She stood in the middle of the yard bathed in moonlight and bowed her head. Then, slowly, she walked into the little blue cottage with the pink shutters, the moon on her back. She never saw the figure watching her from the shadows.

# CHAPTER FORTY-ONE

"MAY I HELP you?"

The woman jumped slightly and looked up at Anne. "Oh! You startled me! I just love these quaint little small town local book shops. Even out here in the sticks you have the *New York Times* best sellers." She scanned the room. "Well, some of them at least."

Anne barely managed a half smile. "Indeed. Let me know if I can help you find anything."

"Oh, I should be fine. You don't have so many books that I'd get lost here." She turned back to the shelf of local authors, dismissing Anne with a wave of her hand.

Anne sat down at her desk, flanked at either end by an antique cash register and her laptop. At least the woman seemed to be looking at the bookshelves. Some days the bookstore traffic was sparse. The story hours and local history talks brought in some tourists, but it was the café that consistently brought in a crowd, both of tourists and locals. And Vince's new burnt sugar concoction was getting rave reviews, even a positive comment from the weekly newspaper food critic.

Anne studied the woman from across the room. She wasn't local, Anne was sure of that. Her clothes were expensive and far too fussy for what the woman called the sticks. And hair like hers required time and hair care products that most Moon Beach folks preferred to do without.

Still, Anne felt there was something vaguely familiar about the woman. She just didn't know what it was. Maybe it would come to her later.

"Oh!" The woman noticed the display case full of pastries in the next room and squealed with delight.

Anne watched as she grabbed one and stuffed the entire cake in her mouth. After she swallowed, she turned to Anne.

"These look delicious. May I try one?" Cream filling stuck to her upper lip.

Anne nodded. The woman selected another and ate it, this time taking the time and effort to chew it before swallowing.

"Goodness gracious! They are good. Do you mind telling me where you get them?"

Anne did mind. "Just someone quaint and small town local."

"Oh, but I simply must have the recipe. That filling is unbelievable."

Anne rarely disliked a person at first sight, but she made an exception in this case. "I'm afraid that won't be possible. It's a proprietary recipe exclusive to the Words & More Café." Darned if she'd give this woman the time of day, let alone Vince's burnt sugar ricotta recipe.

"That'll be five dollars. For the pastry you're eating now and the one you polished off when you first came in."

The woman pursed her lips. "Hmmph." She threw some bills on the table and walked out.

Anne glanced down at the money. Two dollars.

No wonder the woman could afford to wear five hundred dollar shoes.

# CHAPTER FORTY-TWO

"WHERE'S LIZZIE?" VINCE walked into Words & More balancing two trays of pastries. Her car hadn't been parked in front of her little periwinkle cottage when he left Whispering Pines. He assumed she'd be at the bookstore.

Anne looked up from her desk and a sheaf of papers. "Out of town. She said she had some kind of business to take care of." She looked back down at the pile of bills and got to work again.

Vince's head spun as he loaded pastries into the cooler display case.

Anne looked up at him. "You okay? You look a little gray."

"I'm fine. I'm just, uh, surprised that Lizzie's gone."

Anne's eyes flashed concern, maybe a hint of irritation. "Well, Moon Beach may feel like the center of the universe sometimes, but there is an outside world. Speaking of the outside world, get ready." Anne nodded toward the front window, where Vince could see the Senior Center bus pull up in front and a half-dozen tiny white haired women step off the bus.

For the next half hour, Vince enjoyed hearing how wonderful his burnt sugar cannoli and other desserts were as the ladies sucked down an impressive number of pastries.

By the time they left, the dessert case was empty and a bus load of contented and sugar-fueled octogenarians headed home with visions of sugar plums, or at least burnt sugar ricotta cannoli, dancing in their heads.

Anne looked up from the cash register and summarized the recent sales. "Four of them bought that hot erotic series that's big now. The whole boxed set! Then there were two grisly spy thrillers and one steampunk." She laughed. "So much for what I thought our senior citizens were interested in reading. Looks like they want naughty, really naughty, these days. Looks like they came in with quite an appetite for dessert, too, eh? They pretty much cleaned us out."

The addition of the café brought more customers, and more book sales, into Words & More. When Jack and Vince first arrived in Moon Beach, the bookstore had been teetering on the edge financially. Jack had seen that as soon as he examined the financial records. And Vince could see it in the worried look that often crossed Anne's face when she tallied sales at the end of the day.

Recently, though, the influx of new customers kept Anne busy at the cash register throughout the day and her worried look was often replaced by a smile.

Vince was grateful that his contributions were helping to drive more traffic into Words & More, and grateful that he'd had a diversion for the last hour. But now that the Senior Center bus was gone, he started fixating on Lizzie again.

Where had she gone? Was she coming back? Vince's chest was so tight he had trouble breathing.

He'd just assumed she'd be here as part of the Moon Beach community he'd come to know and love. He'd been lulled by the sleepy comfort of Moon Beach, even after Blankenship showed up to remind them all that comfort could be an illusion.

He thought of Ernestine's questions to him and the answer suddenly became clear. Vince wanted to kick himself. He'd spent too much of his life watching it pass him by. Now, somehow, he'd landed in paradise and he still felt like a bystander. He hadn't had a lot of recent experience with relationships; there was no opportunity when Tony was running his life. But now Tony was gone and Vince was on his own. The only thing stopping him was his own inertia.

He'd been sleepwalking, waiting for something to happen instead of making it happen. Why hadn't he told Lizzie how he felt? Why hadn't he been able to figure it out for himself until now, when she was gone?

When she came back to Moon Beach, he would tell her exactly how he felt, if he could sort it out.

What was the worst thing that could happen if he was honest with her?

# CHAPTER FORTY-THREE

LIZZIE'S HANDS TREMBLED when she pulled the delicate old papers out of the envelope and set them on her kitchen table. She had the opportunity here to help Ernestine keep her home, but at the same time she knew she was breaking the law by tampering with public records.

Still, it seemed worth the risk. It wasn't like she'd never done this before. She was good at it. At a time when many young people finished college saddled with student debt, Lizzie not only finished debt free, but with a substantial nest egg tucked away to start her post-college life. She'd majored in art and realized early on her chances of supporting herself with her art alone were slim. The courses she took in art restoration and conservation turned out to be an economic boon for her: she'd been able to turn her new knowledge into a highly marketable skill altering legal documents with a level of proficiency that would have taken a National Security Agency team to detect as fake.

She'd only done it for causes and people she'd believed

had been treated unfairly: powerless underdogs who were getting screwed by big business, big landlord, or big greed. Certainly Ernestine's case fell into that last category.

She opened her yellow plastic tool box and got to work. Some careful cutting, pasting, bleaching, forging, and before long, the new deed was ready to go. She examined her work critically. Yes, it looked good: a dated, registered deed showing transfer of property from Elrod Wilson to Ernestine Castleton.

Her field trip to the Anderton County offices had paid off. In the dusty records office where old records were being fumigated, she'd found a copy of a deed, well-chewed by ancient silverfish, for a tiny strip of land the state had taken by eminent domain to build the new road after the double hurricanes. Lizzie hoped Ernestine had been right: people were happy to leave the area back then and happy to get whatever the state would give them, in this case a tiny strip of land that would be the right of way for the new road. A deed nobody would be likely to contest or even remember. A deed with a date long pre-dating Blankenship's takeover bid.

There was still the pesky issue of how to alter the main registry of deeds ledger to reflect the changes Lizzie had just made. And, of course, the issue of what would happen to her if she got caught.

She had to hope no one would ever look at the deed too closely or figure out her role in altering it. Stopping Blankenship before Ernestine's new deed even surfaced was their best bet.

They needed Blankenship's attention elsewhere, far away from Ernestine and her property. But if that didn't work, this piece of paper might be in the spotlight.

Lizzie's eyes ached from the close work and her nose and throat burned from inhaling dust and old pesticide at the records office. She stretched the kinks out of her back. It had been a long day and she was ready for a good night's sleep. Still, she wanted some reassurance that this was the way to go. She stood up and headed to Bernie for advice.

"Can I ask you a question?"

Bernie looked at Lizzie. "Sure. Fire away."

"I need your, uh, professional opinion. For a hypothetical situation, that is. I mean, I need your opinion in a visual way, not a legal way." Lizzie stammered as she spoke.

Bernie looked at her more closely. "Okay, now I'm intrigued. Shoot."

She handed him a piece of yellowed paper. "If you saw something like this, would you, uh, give it a second thought?"

"Why should I even give it a first thought? Tell me that first and then we'll see."

"Well, let's say, and remember, this is only hypothetical, if you were doing a title search on a property, would you have a problem with this document?"

Bernie looked at Lizzie for a long time before even glancing at the document she'd handed him.

"Listen. I know you want to help Ernestine. I do too. At a glance, this looks great. And no, I would not question it if I saw it during a routine title search. But I know, ah, some of the history here. I doubt this is authentic and you just happened to find the deed to Ernestine's property when she already said she didn't have one."

He squinted and examined the document closely.

"That said, I'm impressed. You do this?"

Lizzie nodded.

"You do good work. I can generally smell a fake, but you'd fool me with this one. You could probably make a fortune forging documents." He looked at her again.

"Maybe you already do. But not here, and not with this one. Let's say Blankenship really does have a bunch of heavy hitters backing him. Most of the major environmental groups have legal teams geared to take on entities like the big oil companies. They would shred this deed, and you as well, my dear, if they thought they could prove it was bogus. This isn't the way to go."

"So what is? I can't bear to think of that slimewad getting his fists on Ernestine's property." The heady scent of the orchids in Ernestine's living room wafted through Lizzie's memory.

"None of us can. But don't go swimming out of your depth here. Let me keep working the legal issues. Your best bet is to help convince Blankenship that he really doesn't want any part of Moon Beach."

"Convince him? What do you mean? Blackmail?"

"Lizzie, you have quite a devious mind. I like that in a person. But no blackmail. Not on your part, at least. He needs to decide that Moon Beach simply isn't worth his effort. Maybe the people, maybe his endangered species, maybe something else can get him to turn on his tail and run from the coast as fast and as far as he can.

"If I know Ernestine, she's already cooking up some kind of voodoo to send him on his way. But I'll bet she could use some some live action help."

"Like what?"

"Look, if you can think up stuff like this," Bernie waved

the deed at Lizzie, "you ought to be able to come up with some other fabricated story that sets Blankenship's wheels spinning. You might want to enlist the aid of your buddy Vince, if you can pull him away from the kitchen long enough. I'll bet he can help you come up with some ideas that'll blow Blankenship away."

Lizzie's eyes lit up. This was beginning to sound like fun.

# CHAPTER FORTY-FOUR

VINCE LOOKED UP from the steering wheel just in time to see the pickup truck turn the corner, its big chrome pipes thrust out at least a foot beyond the rear bumper. The vibration from the souped-up muffler reverberated in his ears as the truck sped off.

Damn, people paid extra to make that much noise. Vince had spent enough, or perhaps too much, time jostling with crowds around Jersey so the sleepy quiet of Moon Beach was sweet music to him. If any vehicle of his ever sounded like that truck, he'd be waiting in line first thing in the morning for Mickey the Muffler Man to open.

He turned up the radio. Nothing like a little classic Jimmy Buffett to drown out those bad vibes. By the time Vince pulled into the Moon Beach shopping center and parked, he was singing about changes in latitude at the top of his lungs.

His attitude changed as soon as he walked into the crowded grocery store. Checkout lines snaked across the front of the store. If he hadn't absolutely needed eggs and butter he would have turned on his heel and headed out.

But the Senior Center crowd was scheduled to come in to Words & More again tomorrow and he knew they would be expecting their sugar rush. He didn't want to disappoint them. The dairy aisle was in the back corner of the store and it took forever to weave through the maze of shopping carts to pick up what he needed and head back to the front of the store.

The express lanes were closed and a coupon queen was hogging one of the two open cash registers. She had loaded her cart so a mountain of bulk goods mushroomed over the top. The entire mountain threatened to cascade onto the floor as the delicate balance changed each time the clerk plucked an item out for scanning.

The customer had a coupon, sometimes two, for every damn item in the cart. The teenage clerk was working hard to keep from crying as she watched the woman select her coupons from the thick loose-leaf notebook she kept propped on the handle of the cart.

People in line glared at the slow-moving scene and muttered to themselves.

"Bitch."

"Who does she think she is? The whole damn world has to slow down so she can save a nickel."

Where was the manager, for crying out loud? At this rate, Vince would be here all afternoon. At last. A man in a necktie with the store logo on it shuffled over to the express lanes and turned on a light. Instantly, a crowd of shoppers carrying small baskets with one or two items in them scrambled like fiddler crabs at the tideline over to the express lane.

Vince moved fast, but not fast enough. He found himself standing in line behind a giant. The guy was six-five, maybe six-six and too thick to be a basketball player. He carried a bottle of wine and a huge bouquet of flowers that had been treated with dye to produce garish unnatural colors. Vince wondered why anyone would buy those things. The real thing struck him as so much better.

"That'll be $87.65." The big guy peeled a crisp hundred dollar bill from a fat wad of bills held together by a wide rubber band. Holy shit. Vince had no idea you could spend that much on a bottle of wine at the grocery store. Guy must have a really hot date.

Vince handed the clerk a twenty for the eggs and butter and headed to the parking lot with his groceries. Neon flower man's head bobbed above the vehicles in the parking lot until it disappeared into that noisy pickup truck.

Vince could see the yellow flames painted on the side as the truck backed out of the parking spot. Its New Jersey license plate gave him a quick start and an uncomfortable reminder of the past.

Just another reason to be grateful for the peace and quiet of Moon Beach. He pulled into the gas station at the edge of the shopping center to fill up before making his way back to Whispering Pines. Buffett was still singing when Vince got back on the road and so he joined in on the chorus. He felt good breathing in the salt air through the open windows.

Until he turned into the long driveway to Whispering Pines.

The New Jersey pickup truck with the yellow flames and the big chrome pipes was parked on the gravel.

Directly in front of Lizzie's cottage.

Vince stumbled into his own cottage and collapsed onto

a kitchen chair. Was this guy the "business" she'd gone out of town for?

Of course Lizzie had a life of her own outside Moon Beach. Why wouldn't she? Just because he was running from his past didn't mean everyone else was, especially not someone like Lizzie. Of course she would have friends, a boyfriend even. But a goon who'd spend money on spray-painted flowers?

Vince imagined him handing the bouquet to Lizzie. What was she thinking? What did she say?

Had they already started in on that pricey bottle of wine?

It was none of Vince's damn business what was happening in Lizzie's little periwinkle cottage. She had her own life and he had–nothing.

All he knew was that, suddenly, breathing had become almost impossible for him.

# CHAPTER FORTY-FIVE

"WHAT THE HELL are you doing here?"

"Nice to see you, too, Lizzie." Marcos smiled as if he had just made a joke. "I missed you. Here." He thrust his big paw and a bunch of neon flowers, already wilting, at her face.

"You're crushing the damn stems." But she took the flowers and walked toward her tiny kitchen. She rummaged through the recycling bin for a pickle jar and filled it with water. Only then did she look at him.

"Thank you. I guess."

"Aren't you supposed to put an aspirin in the water to perk them up or something?"

"Anyone gets an aspirin, it's gonna be me. You're here two minutes and already I've got a splitting headache. What do you want?"

"I missed you, baby."

Lizzie shuddered. He'd never called her "baby" before. It sounded both menacing and incongruous coming from this man who in the past had said too little to her until it had been far too late.

Marcos cocked his head sideways like a puppy looking for a treat. But with an undersized fedora sliding off his oversized head, the effect was macabre rather than adorable.

"You hurt me, baby."

"How did I hurt you? And stop calling me baby. You surprised me, that's all. Like just showing up here now. Like giving me that—" she stopped and shook her head. "I wasn't expecting any of it. I don't do well with surprises."

Lizzie wished he'd been as menacing when they first met as he appeared to her now. They'd been lab partners in the art school welding class and they shared an interest in creating art from hunks of scrap metal. But if Marcos had a vision in his head of what his art could look like, it got lost in the transition from idea to welded metal. His work was clumsy, undefined.

Lizzie, on the other hand, imagined soaring delicate sculptures rising out of a pile of junk. She knew exactly how and where to join the metal pieces together to create something beautiful, something unique.

What she couldn't do was lug around pieces of scrap metal that were larger than she was. Marcos had volunteered, gladly at first, to help her, and so their odd partnership began. Marcos's size and bench pressing abilities served him far better than his artistic vision. For a while it was fun, at least for Lizzie.

She was able to build her visions with the help of Marcos's muscle power. Visions that came alive in scrap metal as edgy and graceful, and that changed as a viewer walked around the constructions.

Their Big/Junk/Art show had opened to rave reviews and even resulted in several sales at the opening reception.

Lizzie sailed through opening night in a haze of success, heady from praise and the fleeting glimmer of fame. By her fourth glass of champagne she was giddy. Later on she would remember singing, dancing, and not enough else.

The next day, Marcos arrived at her door with a small cardboard box in his hand, and he thrust it at her much as he had just done with the bouquet of flowers.

Lizzie frowned. She didn't have anything for Marcos and hadn't really thought there'd been a reason to exchange gifts. Their success the night before seemed like enough of a present.

"You gonna open it?" She'd fumbled with the box, hoping it was some gag gift, though Marcos had never seemed the type for jokes. Or maybe it was the cash from the sales. She became uneasy as she unwrapped the folded tissue paper and felt what was inside.

It was a ring. Ornate, heavy, with a large purple stone. Lizzie's heart sank.

"You like it?"

She burst into tears. "Oh no, Marcos. Not me. Not you. Not now." Not ever is what she'd needed to add.

By morning, Marcos was gone, his workshop and apartment empty. He'd taken every piece from the Big/Junk/Art show, along with all the money they'd made from sales at the show.

Two weeks later, Lizzie arrived in Moon Beach.

There was probably some unfinished business between them now that they stood face to face once again.

"Marcos, look. I'm sorry about everything that happened. I had no idea you thought I was, well, whatever you thought I was." Lizzie's mind raced trying to come up with the right word. "I'm not that. I'm just a friend. A fellow artist." A schmuck and an idiot if somehow I led you on.

Marcos frowned. "But we had fun together, Lizzie. Nobody else ever laughed and joked with me the way you do. We make beautiful art together. Don't you see? We're connected in a special way." He moved closer to her.

Lizzie backed away. "Look, our art stuff together was fun, sure. And we can be friends. But that's it. Just friends."

"The night of the reception. We were more than just friends then, weren't we?"

Lizzie looked at him blankly. What had happened that night? She vaguely remembered hugging and kissing some of her artist friends who'd come to the reception. Had she kissed Marcos as well? Probably. Even worse, had she slept with him? She shuddered at the thought.

"Marcos, to tell you the truth, I don't remember very much about that night. I had too much to drink and I, ah, may have said or done things I probably shouldn't have. I'm sorry." She stared at her feet.

"Son of a fucking bitch." His voice was low, guttural. Lizzie looked up again.

His face scared Lizzie. She'd had no idea how threatening he could be. She remembered her friends, her father, trying to discourage her from working with Marcos. They must have seen what she hadn't been able to recognize until this minute.

With a sinking heart she realized she'd thought more about herself and her own need to have someone help her with her art than about Marcos's feelings. Had she led him on? Certainly he had misread their casual friendship as something more. She'd hurt him, hurt him terribly.

Right then, she resolved to keep her guard up, to not let anyone get too close. If she'd been more careful, Marcos would not be standing there in her kitchen while she stood trembling a few feet away.

"Listen, I owe you an apology. I'm really sorry about, well, about everything. That you think I led you on. That you got hurt. That I hurt you. I'm just so sorry."

His face remained a dark mask. "Yeah. Well, I'll just be on my way then." He turned abruptly and headed out the door.

It took forever for his big truck tires to crunch over the gravel and finally hit the road.

Lizzie turned the lightweight bolt on her front door and a minute later shoved the kitchen table across the door frame. She pushed a heavy upholstered chair up against the table and flopped into it.

Only then did she begin to breathe again.

# CHAPTER FORTY-SIX

VINCE COULDN'T SLEEP, even after he heard the big truck pull out of Whispering Pines. Had Jersey Man left by himself? Or did Lizzie go with him?

By dawn, Vince gave up and headed into the kitchen. If he couldn't sleep, he might as well try to bake something. He decided on cinnamon rolls and spent far too long slamming the yeasty dough with his fists. He stopped kneading the dough only when his knuckles hurt.

By the time the rolls came out of the oven it was light outside. He drizzled sweet icing on them and dug into one, still steaming hot.

He almost broke a tooth. Over-kneading had made the rolls tough, certainly too tough for Words & More. But dipped in coffee they weren't bad, and definitely easier on the teeth.

The rolls gave him the excuse he wanted to head over to Lizzie's cottage. She was always willing to test drive his concoctions, as she put it, and offer her opinion. He selected the best looking rolls, put them on a plate, and headed across the gravel drive.

He looked at her car. She certainly wasn't going anywhere soon. He picked up the envelope stuck in Lizzie's front door and knocked.

"I made some cinnamon rolls, but they didn't turn out so hot. Definitely not good enough for the café. If you dunk them in your coffee they're okay, though." He talked faster and more than he had intended, but he couldn't slow down.

"They smell delicious. Come on in." Lizzie's eyes were red and swollen.

"I found this on your doorstep." Vince tried to sound casual as he handed Lizzie the envelope.

He'd also tried not to read what was written on the envelope, but couldn't help himself. The bold scrawl read: "You don't owe me nothing."

She frowned as she took the envelope and opened it. Six one-hundred dollar bills fell out onto the table. She picked up the bills and stacked them carefully so Benjamin Franklin was facing the same way on all of them, then placed them back in the envelope.

She looked at Vince. "You want some coffee?" She'd already pulled two mugs out of the cabinet and started pouring. Her hands were shaking and coffee splashed on the table. She moved the envelope onto the counter away from the spilled coffee.

"I see what you mean about the rolls. All Anne would need is a lawsuit from someone breaking a tooth on one of these little rocks. It'd keep Bernie busy for a while." She tried to laugh, but it came out sounding forced. "They taste pretty good, though." She set her mug down since her hands were still shaking and more coffee was spilling on the table.

"Lizzie?"

"Yeah?"

"Your tires are flat. All four of them." Bastard must have used an ice pick.

She sighed. "I guess Marcos is right then. I don't owe him nothing."

She blew her nose into a dish towel, then wiped the tears that started exploding down her face.

Vince stood up, uncertain whether he should stay.

Lizzie motioned toward the chair. "You didn't finish your coffee yet."

He sat back down. Did she want to say something? Did he? Neither of them spoke while they drank their coffee. Finally Lizzie broke the silence.

"Oh, man." She rubbed her watery eyes and looked at Vince. "I am the biggest fuck-up in the entire world. Loser, user, abuser. You don't want to know me."

Somehow, this didn't seem like the right time for Vince to tell Lizzie how he felt about her.

And at this point, he wasn't even sure himself.

# CHAPTER FORTY-SEVEN

JACK WALKED INTO the photography studio and looked around at his fellow students. Some sported expensive cameras and khaki vests with more pockets than Jack had gadgets to put in them. He looked down at his little digital camera and wondered if he was in the wrong place. Well, screw it, if he was. If the breath-taking color photos lining the walls of the studio were any indication of what he might learn in the class, he was staying. He was ready to start breathing again.

A hush fell on the room as a tiny woman strode from the back of the studio and leaned against the gleaming Parsons table in the middle of the room. Her short gray hair was streaked with purple and red highlights. Small red beads dangled from the end of each silver ear wire.

"Welcome to Fresh Eyes 101! I'm Elaine Davidson and I'm glad you're here." She looked around at the eight people in front of her. "We're going to use our time in this workshop to look at the world with fresh eyes. A simple point-and-shoot camera will work for that just as well as a $40,000 Hasselblad. It's your vision that will change."

Within minutes, Elaine had everyone outside on an assignment: as many shots of the parking lot and its two palm trees as they could take in ten minutes.

"So we came all this way just to take pictures of concrete?" A man with expensive gear grumbled to his wife as she knelt on the pavement to get another shot.

"Hey, your camera looks like mine." The young woman standing in front of Jack held a small red Nikon, similar to his blue one. She stuck out her hand. "I'm Mallory." Her grip was strong, self-assured. Her unruly dark hair was pulled back into a long braid and her welcoming smile was approachable.

"Jack here."

Mallory looked vaguely familiar to Jack, but so many young women Lizzie's age did. His thoughts drifted to Lizzie and he breathed a sigh of relief that she was nearby, safe in Moon Beach.

"Ten minutes!" Elaine's voice jolted him back to the parking lot. For such a small person, Elaine had a commanding presence. She began herding people into the studio and downloading their photos.

Half an hour later, the class had viewed hundreds of pictures of palm trees and the parking lot on Elaine's large projection screen. Jack's mind swelled from seeing the different ways these seemingly mundane objects could be viewed. His vision was definitely changing. Elaine moved fast. She was already on to the next assignment. The group headed outdoors again and to the nearby park.

"Why are you looking at me like that?" Mallory's voice broke into Jack's concentration.

"Sorry. I was just thinking you reminded me of someone. Probably one of my daughter's friends. She's about your age." Jack changed the subject. "What brought you to Elaine's class?"

"The second I saw Elaine's photographs, I fell in love. I thought this workshop would help my work. Y'know, fresh eyes and all that. I'm a graphic designer. My company does a lot of environmental promotion as well as work with real estate developers." She laughed. "Kind of like working both sides of the aisle, I guess. Oh, look!" A butterfly landed on a nearby vine. Mallory headed toward it with her camera.

For the next half hour, Jack focused on his camera and Elaine's directions. She was pushing them to stretch themselves, and it felt great.

It was dark by the time he pulled into Whispering Pines. And damned if Elaine hadn't given them an assignment to take pictures at sunrise. He heard laughter up on Bernie's and Anne's deck, and both Lizzie's and Vince's voices. The tinkling of glasses, then Bernie said, "Come on up for a nightcap."

The invitation was a welcome way to end a long day. Jack headed up the steps to the deck and stared at Anne.

No wonder Mallory looked familiar.

# CHAPTER FORTY-EIGHT

VINCE SENSED DANGER as soon as he stepped into the cottage. A heavy sweet scent set the hairs on the back of his neck straight out and his whole body on high alert. The metallic taste of fear bubbled up in his throat and his heart started pounding.

For all he knew the intruder or, worse yet, intruders were still inside. He grabbed the big conch shell they used as a doorstop. Not quite brass knuckles, but it would have to do. He turned slowly.

The kitchen had been ransacked. Cupboard doors, gleaming white in the late afternoon sun, hung open; a ceramic canister lay tipped on its side on the counter, covered with a dusty haze of flour. Vince's neatly organized file folders and cookbooks were scattered across the kitchen table and on the floor. His laptop lay open on the table.

Tony. Vince's heart sank. Vince was sure his father had left behind plenty of hard feelings when he died. Hard feelings in Tony's world generally led to an unfortunate end for someone. A twenty-foot walk off a ten-foot pier,

189

Tony used to say with a savage laugh.

Had someone traced Vince here, maybe followed Tony and Shirley when they'd come looking for him? Or seen him when he'd visited Tony that last time? His mind flashed on that big black pickup truck squealing toward Royal Palm Breeze when Tony's body was still warm.

Tony was past the point of resolving any unfinished business by then. But Vince wasn't. What if someone wanted to get belated revenge on Tony by targeting Vince?

It was unfair, but that was how things worked in Tony's universe. Unfinished business that started in the family stayed in the family. And Vince, unfortunately, was still family.

Family. Vince thought about his new friends, his Moon Beach family. The image of Lizzie, with her tangled copper hair and hearty laugh, then Lizzie, sobbing into her dish towel, swept across his field of vision. Ernestine followed, with her blue veined hands wrapped around her walking stick. Ernestine, chanting mumbo-jumbo under the full moon to try to save her home while Vince was taking a late night run.

Vince fought nausea at the thought of putting them in danger. This was the downside to carving out a real life for himself. With the success of the Words & More Café, he'd become too public. If someone really wanted to find him, he was an easy target.

Tony's thugs might be right here, now, in the lemon yellow cottage at Whispering Pines. Vince's bedroom door was shut. What if someone was lurking behind that closed door waiting for him?

He looked down at the conch shell. For an instant

Vince wished he'd been more his father's son. Maybe Tony had been right to carry a Glock wherever he went, even to the bathroom. Especially to the bathroom. He used to make the same joke over and over about not getting caught with your pants down.

Now Vince understood what Tony meant. He put down the clumsy shell, grabbed a different weapon, and crept down the hallway. He felt like he was walking down that ten-foot pier himself.

Vince paused before the bedroom door. Time to step off the pier. He flung the door open so hard the doorknob gouged the plaster as it hit the wall behind it.

Nothing. Nobody.

The windows were still latched from the inside and the little closet held only clothes and a pair of flip-flops. Vince knelt down to check under the bed. Dust motes and a lone sock.

He froze on his knees when he heard a door open behind him.

Vince scrambled to his feet when he heard Lizzie call his name from the living room. He raced into the hallway and bumped directly into her.

She backed up. "What the hell's going on?"

Vince looked down. Sticky red liquid dribbled down his arm and onto the floor. A trail of red led from the bedroom to where he stood. Vince tried a weak grin. He was too relieved to care how silly he looked clutching the squirt bottle of hot pepper sauce.

"Someone broke into the cottage. I thought they might still be inside." He looked at the bottle. "I didn't know what else to grab. I figured I could go for someone's eyes with it and at least slow them down."

He tried to smile again. "Or else they'd die laughing from how ridiculous I look. I should have grabbed one of your dad's chicken costumes instead." He hoped his tone was light enough to fool her.

Lizzie broke into her familiar deep laugh. "Vince, what kind of a hit man are you? Think you can take out the mob with a couple of chili peppers? You're dreaming."

Vince hurried to the kitchen sink so she couldn't see his face. Lizzie had nailed it, and him, with just a few words. "I want to clean up this mess before tracking it around too much." He grabbed a sponge and retraced his walk, wiping up the sauce as he moved.

His adrenalin was still pumping, but a sense of relief washed over him as well. This was the first time he'd heard Lizzie laugh since Marcos's visit, and the first time they'd been together without a heavy awkwardness separating them. Maybe Vince did owe something to Tony after all.

They moved through the cottage to assess the damage, but it appeared only the kitchen had been hit.

"That's weird," Lizzie said. "My dad's new camera is just sitting there on his dresser. He'd be bullshit if he lost it now, just when he's so into that photography class of his. And your laptop's on the table. Whoever came in, something must have scared them before they got to take anything valuable."

She giggled. "Unless your hand-milled pastry flour is worth its weight in gold. Which it just might be."

Later that night, Vince tossed and turned for hours, unable to sleep. Lizzie had called it like it was; he was totally unprepared to face whatever demons might be chasing him. And he certainly wasn't doing anything to chase away demons like Blankenship.

The break-in was the kick he needed to get off his butt. If someone from Tony's past had come looking for revenge, Vince needed to take care of business now, before they showed up again. Vince had vowed to do whatever it took to save Ernestine's home. But had he done anything so far to help her? He'd let Marcos and those damn neon flowers get in the way for too long.

Whatever it took.

If he was dreaming, he might as well dream big. Even if the dream turned into a plan that was probably illegal, definitely dangerous, and ultimately left a huge amount to both chance and luck. What did he have to lose?

Practically everything, if he dared to be honest with himself. But a crazy plan was all he could come up with, and maybe doing something, anything, was better than doing nothing.

When he finally drifted off to sleep, it was to the remembered sound of Lizzie's rich, open laugh as they stood together in the hallway.

He was still smiling when he woke up in the morning.

# CHAPTER FORTY-NINE

"DO YOU STILL want to help save Ernestine?" Vince's question seemed to surprise Lizzie.

"Jeez, Vince, what do you think? Of course I do. Especially if it means doing the dirty on that rat Blankenship."

"We've got to convince Blankenship his whole scheme is more trouble than it's worth," Vince said. "He'll never let Ernestine's property go out of the goodness of his heart."

"That's what Bernie said too."

"Bernie? What do you mean?"

"I had this crazy idea I could come up with a fake deed for Ernestine and solve everything with that." Lizzie shook her head. "Fat chance."

"Oh?" The morning was full of surprises.

"I ran it by Bernie to get his legal opinion."

"What'd he say?"

"He said I should drop it." She grinned at him. "He also said I should team up with you to go after Blankenship."

"Smart man." Vince grinned back at her. "I'd like to make life so damn miserable for Blankenship that he'll split on his own. Decide that ruining Moon Beach isn't worth whatever moolah he thinks he can pull out of it."

"Going after the guy with a bottle of hot sauce isn't going to work," Lizzie said.

"No, but I've been thinking about what could work. We just might be able to blast Blankenship out of town for good."

"How?"

"I've got, uh, some experience with explosives." He shrugged. "I guess it's part of Tony's legacy to me." For an instant his mind flashed back to black smoke seen from the rear view mirror of Tony's SUV. "I'd like to lure Blankenship someplace where we could set up an explosion or two to go off all around him. Just to scare him. Give him an idea of how we could blow up whatever he has in mind for Moon Beach," he said.

Lizzie started to say something but Vince kept going. "It'd basically just be fireworks, nothing dangerous. But Blankenship wouldn't know that. I'm pretty good at making explosions look convincing. Lots of noise and smoke, but no real damage." He didn't think Lizzie needed to know the full extent of his experience.

Vince's plan sounded even sketchier in the light of day than it had in the middle of the night. They'd have to get Blankenship to show up somewhere, blow something up, and make sure no one got hurt or arrested in the process.

"What do you think?" Vince talked fast, too fast, not giving Lizzie an opportunity to point out the many holes in the plan.

"I think you're crazy," Lizzie said. No one had ever

called him crazy before, and Vince realized with a start it sounded good to him.

"That may be. Otherwise I'd never even dream of anything like this. Are you in?"

"Of course. But where can we go?"

"I'd like to get as far from Moon Beach as possible." If any of Tony's buddies were to recognize Vince's signature explosion technique, he'd hate to see them recognize it too close to Moon Beach. "There are a bunch of deserted shopping malls all over the state. Maybe one of those, if we could lure him there." Vince imagined setting small dynamite and fireworks charges in an abandoned Piggly Wiggly parking lot if they could figure out how to get Blankenship there.

Lizzie scrunched her face in concentration for a minute. Then her eyes opened wide. "Vince! I've got it!"

He shook his head in disbelief as she told him her idea.

"A junkyard? How could we convince Blankenship to head to a junkyard?"

"Easy-schmeasy. I'm really good at faking documents. Even Bernie said so. I can come up with a business proposal and a bunch of snazzy prospectus things. We'll make Blankenship think he's gonna meet with a bunch of suits just itching to hand him money. I, uh, have some stuff left over from an old job I can use as a model. And Rennie's is perfect. It's in a god-forsaken industrial park a couple of hours inland. It was my go-to place to get scrap metal for my sculptures."

She pantomimed opening a beer can and drinking. "Rennie's almost never there, anyway. Pretty much works by appointment, if you can believe it. He spends more time on a barstool than at the junkyard."

Vince stared at her. Lizzie seemed to know the regular drinking habits of a junkyard owner. She had an arsenal of forgery skills at her command. The plan, and Lizzie, were getting more complicated by the minute. Somehow he found that appealing. And possibly dangerous.

"This whole thing has more holes than a truckload of Swiss cheese," he said.

"But it's a shot at helping Ernestine. We can always figure out how to fill in the holes as we go along."

"The holes are what worry me. We might just fall in one and not be able to crawl out," he said. Vince thought back to his first morning on Moon Beach when he met Ernestine walking along the beach. He still had the little shell she'd given him then.

They would not let Ernestine lose her home. At least not without a fight, even a fight filled with potholes and fuck-up potential. With a sidekick like Lizzie, the preposterous scheme seemed almost reasonable to Vince. It also sounded like it could be a hell of a lot of fun.

He smiled. "Let's do it. Rennie's it is."

The likelihood of trouble seemed a distant possibility instead of a sure thing.

# CHAPTER FIFTY

BERNIE EASED HIS reluctant feet into the wingtips. The shoes and the pinstripe suit felt as phony as the chicken suits, and a hell of a lot less fun. He stuffed Spence's report and his own investigative efforts into a leather folder. He was ready for Blankenship.

Blankenship's office was located in a nondescript one story building on the road to Anderton. According to the directory in the front hallway, two accountants, a rental management company, and an insurance agent shared space in the building with Green Eco-Tours. The large For Lease signs in the lobby and the parking lot suggested many of the doors along the dingy corridor opened to empty offices and cheap rents.

Bernie tapped on the door and waited until Blankenship said, "Come in."

The office appeared to be furnished with whatever the former tenants had left behind. Bernie moved a stained upholstered chair from the corner until it was positioned directly across the big desk from Blankenship. He sat down. The two men stared at each other for a good twenty seconds before Bernie started speaking.

"Look. I'll make this quick. You haven't got a chance in hell of grabbing Ms. Castleton's property," he said. "Green Eco-Tours is as bogus as you are. You haven't filed a lick of paperwork for this enterprise. Not as a corporation, not as a non-profit, nothing. How you got as far as you did with Friends of the Wild and your private partners is a mystery to me. But it's irrelevant since it's not going any farther. You try to put in a bid for Ms. Castleton's land and the appeal process will be in motion so fast your head will spin. I guarantee it'll cost you more than you can even dream. And that will be just the beginning."

Blankenship smiled and stood up. "I love a challenge, Simpson. Thanks for stopping by." He pointed toward the door. "Please close it on your way out."

Bernie remained seated in the stained chair. He shuffled through his papers and selected one with WARRANT stamped on the top before looking at Blankenship again. "May I call you Vaughn? Vaughn Browning, that is?" He watched the color drain from Blankenship's face as he sunk back down into his chair.

"Given your criminal record, Mr. Browning, I suspect a great many people would be interested to learn you're doing business here in Moon Beach under a new name, trying to steal an old lady's property and ruin the environment."

"I suggest you drop your money-grabbing scam and get the hell out of town before some of your former colleagues find out where you are," Bernie said.

"Are you threatening me?"

"I wouldn't dream of it. I'm just trying to save us all

some time, money, and aggravation. I hope this is the last I see of you. Good day, Mr. Browning."

Bernie rose and walked to the door. He left it open on his way out.

Blankenship waited until he heard the outside lobby door open and Simpson leave the building. Only then did he walk over to the blasted chair Simpson had been sitting in and knock it on its side. God damn bad luck. The Castleton broad could have had any podunk local for a lawyer and she picked Simpson.

Green Eco-Tours was on the brink of getting new investors to sign on, Blankenship could feel it. How long he could hang around waiting for them? He could barely afford a plane ticket, let alone a whole new life, with the financial commitments he'd been able to snag so far. He'd have to take his chances and stay.

He picked up the chair and moved it back to the corner of the office. He looked around at the room, critically, for the first time. Everything was drab and dirty. He deserved better. Time for him to get it. But he'd better get it fast.

He heard the mailman unlock the row of boxes in the front lobby so he walked down to pick up his bills, pizza ads, and the rest of the junk mail that ended up littering the streets.

The mailman held out a large white envelope: heavy, thick, expensive looking. Blankenship grabbed it and raced back to his office.

He tore open the envelope and grinned as he started reading the letter. Yes! Several individual investors as well as corporate entities were ready to back Green Eco-Tours. Slick corporate brochures and a formal prospectus slid out of the envelope and onto the desk. He'd probably look at those later, but initially his interest was the letter itself, listing the investors and outlining the agenda for an upcoming meeting. A meeting featuring Green Eco-Tours and what he already saw as his new partners.

Blankenship wanted to congratulate himself. His own promotional materials must have looked pretty convincing. He sighed with contentment. This meeting was what he needed to send him on his way.

It seemed like the answer to a prayer.

# CHAPTER FIFTY-ONE

JACK SCRAMBLED TO get out of the way, and just in time. He'd been in line for a direct hit by the heavy camera bag one of his classmates slung angrily over his shoulder. "That's it," the man said. "I've had enough of these amateurs. I thought we'd be dealing with pros in this class." He looked at his wife. "Come on. Let's go."

She got up slowly and followed him to the door. At the threshold she turned and smiled before mouthing "I'll be back" to the rest of the class.

Jack mouthed "good luck" to her as she walked away.

For a moment no one moved.

"Well. I certainly hope Anita will come back. And preferably without Charlie." Elaine leaned against the table and crossed her arms in front of her.

"Let's get back to work, shall we? I want you to work in twos." She grouped people by pairs, then rattled off a new assignment and a thirty minute time limit.

"I liked Anita, y'know? I hope she'll be back," Mallory said to no one in particular as they headed out the door.

Mallory walked with Jack across the parking lot.

"Charlie's probably okay, too. He might just be out of his element here. He reminds me a little of my dad. The gotta be in charge type who freaks out when he can't control everything."

"What do you mean?"

"My dad's a really wonderful guy, but it's hard for him when he can't be in charge. Like he was really opposed to my moving down here. Even though it's a great opportunity for me and the job I had up north was the pits. I think he was afraid he wouldn't be able to control stuff for me somehow." She smiled. "I'm always gonna be Daddy's little girl. And he doesn't want to see me get hurt."

Jack nodded. "I can sure relate to your dad with that one."

"It's hard for my mom sometimes, when my dad makes all the big decisions. Like moving around when I was little and then not wanting to budge since they've retired. Mom would really like it here, I think, but there's something holding them back from even visiting. Almost like they're scared of something. Weird."

She looked at her watch. "We'd better get started. Elaine is a slave driver, but this workshop is more fun than I've had in a long time."

Elaine's assignments were ambiguous and challenging. But Jack was having trouble concentrating on photography when he was thinking about Mallory. How could he even bring up the questions he wanted to ask her?

He knew he should probably just leave well enough alone. Push his thoughts to the back of his mind. Wrap his head around Elaine's current challenge and shoot contradictory images to share with the class. He had to admit, seeing the different ways each person interpreted Elaine's direction in capturing the world around them was exhilarating.

"Hey, do you want to take pictures or what?" Mallory's voice brought him back to the present task and the vacant lot across the street from Elaine's studio. "She wants us to come up with a set of 101 contradictory images, whatever that means, so we should get going. Do I get to contradict you, or do you want to contradict me?" She grinned at him and pushed a wisp of hair away from her face.

Half an hour later the group headed back into the studio and downloaded their photos onto Elaine's computer for a slide show and comment session. Anita slipped in the door and joined them.

"I'm glad you're back," Elaine said. "We're going to view our perceptions of contradictory images. I suspect you are already familiar with the concept." She wrapped the irony in a sympathetic smile and Anita nodded.

"Let's see what we've got here." Elaine directed them to the large projection screen and the first image. For the next half hour, the group commented on what they saw, or didn't see, in the photos.

Elaine snapped the lights back on and sat on the big Parsons table. "You know there's only one more session left in this workshop." There were several audible groans from the class. "This workshop was an experiment for me and I couldn't be happier with how it's come together. I'd love to do a follow-up workshop if enough of you are interested," she said.

"Okay, here's your final assignment. Print your ten favorite photos from this workshop. Then write a short artist's statement to accompany the photos. What you learned about yourself, what you hated about the experience, what you had for dinner last night. Anything that works for you.

"We'll mat the photos and hang them up in the gallery, invite our friends, and party. Sound like a plan?"

Several days later, Jack helped Elaine hang the matted prints on the gallery's creamy walls. The variety of perspectives impressed him. He thought back to their first set of predictable, stilted pictures of palm trees in the parking lot. "These are terrific. So different from our first timid pictures. We learned a lot from you."

Elaine smiled. "I learned a lot from y'all as well. It's fun to see how people can change and grow once they get out of their comfort zones. You think you'd take a second workshop if I offered it?"

"Are you kidding? Sign me up for whatever you've got in mind."

Elaine smiled again. "I'm not sure you're ready for that, Jack. But I'll put you on the list for the next photography workshop."

She was holding one of Mallory's prints, an osprey nest high in a clump of cypress trees. "Hand me the next print, okay? I really love this set."

Jack sucked in a deep breath when he read Mallory's artist statement. He had to tell Mallory about Anne. And Anne about Mallory.

# CHAPTER FIFTY-TWO

ANNE SMOOTHED HER hair back and captured it in a silver clasp. Her hands trembled and a small wisp escaped to curl around her ear.

Bernie looked at her. "You okay?"

"I'm fine. I think." Anne smiled and a small twitch danced across her cheek. "Let's go. I don't want to make us late for Jack's big show."

Five minutes later they were in the driveway. "Ernestine, why don't you ride up front with Bernie? I'll sit in back with Lizzie and Vince if that's okay with everyone," Anne said and opened the back door of the car.

"That's if I can get in the damned thing. You ought to have an elevator lift to hoist folks up." Ernestine complained, but she didn't have any trouble stepping up into the SUV. Her turquoise walking stick matched her flowing caftan. She'd even tossed some turquoise eyeshadow on. "I'm in."

"I haven't seen Dad so excited in years," Lizzie said. "When I was little he took lots of pictures but he kind of slowed down by the time I got to high school. I can hardly wait to see his stuff."

Ernestine stuck Springsteen in the car's CD player within minutes of leaving Whispering Pines.

"You rock!" Lizzie tapped Ernestine's shoulder in time to the music.

"Yeah, well I finally rocked my way up from eight-track to cassettes to CDs and now these fool things are obsolete too. Now it's the damn cloud, whatever that is. It's hard to keep up."

Bernie turned to her and grinned. "You're doing just fine." They were silent for most of the drive from Moon Beach to Anderton and Elaine Davidson's photography studio.

Bernie pulled into the parking lot. Red and purple helium balloons danced above a stone statue that stood next to the front door.

Ernestine led the way to the door with Lizzie and Vince directly behind her. They disappeared into the building and Lizzie's laugh could be heard out on the street.

Anne gripped Bernie's hand and he brushed his lips across her cheek. "Take your time. And you don't have to go in if you don't want to. You can do this later."

"No, I'm going in. Jack said she wanted me to come. Just give me a second." She leaned against the statue and the balloons bounced lightly against her head and back.

"I'm ready."

She paused on the threshold, scanning faces. The room was packed, filled with laughter and conversation.

She took a sharp intake of breath and Bernie looked at her sideways.

"SaraBeth," she whispered, so softly even Bernie could

barely hear it.

Anne walked across the room slowly, ignoring everyone and everything except those eyes and that unruly hair. Finally she stood directly in front of her.

Mallory looked up. Her eyes widened in recognition when she looked at Anne and saw an image of herself reflected there. Tears welled up in her eyes as she said, "You're really here."

"My dearest, I've waited so long for you." Anne's voice cracked and she touched Mallory's wet cheek, then enveloped her in the hug she'd only imagined for more than two decades.

Statement of the Artist, Mallory James:

*Something I can't explain has always beckoned me to the coast. The day I arrived here and first inhaled the salt air, I felt like I'd come home. Walking along the shoreline ignites my soul with both sea spray and wild hope.*

*I have a confession: I came south hoping to find my birth mother. Will I? It almost doesn't matter. I've already found what feels like home here. Anything more would be magic.*

"Holy crap." Lizzie was sniffling by the time she got to the end of Mallory's statement. "She totally hit it. Even if it's just coincidence and not DNA that makes them look like mother and daughter."

"I'll say," Vince added. *I've already found what feels like home here.*

Ernestine wiped a tear from her cheek. "I've been hoping for this for years. But terrified for Anne at the possibility. Terrified it wouldn't happen or work out the way she wanted it to. But look at them grinning at each other. I have a feeling this will be good for both of them."

Vince watched as tears continued to roll down Ernestine's face. Anne's dream was finally coming true while Ernestine's life was turning into a nightmare.

They had to stop Blankenship, and a bad plan was better than no plan. Vince looked at Lizzie.

"Tomorrow's the day," he said.

She nodded. "Tomorrow."

# CHAPTER FIFTY-THREE

AS VINCE LOADED the trunk of the car, he tried not to think about the potential for disaster lurking around the corner. The whole fiasco might put Ernestine in an even worse place than her current predicament.

Lizzie dropped a bag into the trunk next to the boxes Vince had already packed. "That's it!"

Vince shut the trunk carefully and got into the driver's seat. They were as ready as they were going to be. Gravel shot down the drive as he gunned the little car away from the quiet of Whispering Pines and Moon Beach. At least they had new tires, thanks to Marcos.

They rode in silence for a while, each lost in their own doubts and fears.

"Vince?"

"Yeah?"

"Penny for your thoughts?"

"My thoughts aren't worth even that much right now," Vince said. "Best case, this won't work out the way we're hoping. Worst case, we'll be dead and Ernestine will still lose her land."

"You want to head back?" Lizzie's question sounded like a challenge.

Vince slowed down enough to look directly at her for a second. Her eyes were blazing.

"Not on your life." He winced over his choice of words.

A few hours later, Lizzie motioned Vince to pull off the interstate. "This is the exit," she said. They drove for about five miles and watched the landscape change from rolling grassland to suburban development to gritty industrial wasteland.

"That's the place." Lizzie pointed and Vince came to a stop. The rusted sign, almost illegible from time and neglect, read Rennie's Scrap Metal. The sidewalk next to the car was crumbled and uneven with crabgrass and dandelions poking out of the holes in the cement. Barbed wire coiled along the top of the chain link fence.

The entrance gate was closed, but the metal frame had long ago been twisted so that anyone could walk through it and into the junkyard. Piles of scrap metal lay everywhere, and a large corrugated metal shack stood in the middle of the yard. Its walls leaned precariously to one side and the building appeared to be held up more by its contents than by any discernible frame.

Vince whistled. "Jesus H. Christ." He couldn't move.

What had they been thinking?

Lizzie got out of the car. "We don't have a lot of time. Blankenship is supposed to be here in half an hour."

"We better get started," Vince said. He lugged the big boxes out of the trunk and headed for the perimeter of the junkyard. He was sweating and the metallic tang of fear hung in the back of his throat.

It was too late to turn back now. Vince opened the first

box and started pulling out what he needed. He concentrated on his task and tried not to think about what could go wrong. Soon both boxes were empty and everything was in place. He had just finished when he heard a car pull up.

"Vince. Blankenship's here."

Vince looked at his watch. The bastard was early. He scrambled to get up.

Two car doors slammed. Bad news. That meant Blankenship wasn't alone. Blankenship had crawled through the opening in the fence and was walking fast. A young man wearing a green Friends of the Wild T-shirt followed Blankenship into the junkyard.

Blankenship's face was flaming red. "What the fuck is going on here? This ain't no fucking office park." He looked around and scowled at Lizzie.

"What the hell are you doing here? Where's my investor team?" He held out the glossy brochures, the lengthy business prospectus Lizzie had created to lure him to the bogus meeting.

"Son of a motherfucking bitch!" His voice shook with fury. "You think you can con me?" He tossed the papers to the man beside him. "Nobody fucks with my head like that. And gets away with it."

The plan, shaky from the start, started falling apart: Blankenship pulled out a gun.

Lizzie stood ramrod straight in the middle of the junkyard. Her face was deathly pale and two bright red spots stood out on her cheeks.

She stood motionless as Blankenship aimed the small silver weapon directly at her.

Vince raced toward her from the back edge of the yard.

Adrenalin pulsed through his veins and the heavy sweet smell of the dynamite burned his nostrils. He stared transfixed as Blankenship drew the gun in slow motion. Vince's fingers moved just as slowly. Could he will them to function in time?

Vince pressed a button on the remote starter, then lunged before Lizzie had a chance to move. Before Blankenship could pull the trigger.

Two loud explosions cracked at the edge of the property. Blankenship whirled in the direction of the explosions as Vince jumped on him. They both fell to the ground. Blankenship held the gun close to his own chest while Vince clawed blindly, trying to gain purchase of the metal grip. They scuffled across the concrete, tumbling in slow motion, first one on top and then the other.

Vince felt the sharpness of the gun muzzle pressing into his ribcage. He struggled to slip sideways and away from Blankenship's heavy weight as blood pounded through his temples.

Blankenship was on top. Vince was in better physical shape, but Blankenship outweighed him by forty pounds. Vince inched his left hand up to Blankenship's throat and leaned his fist hard against the man's windpipe. If he could only keep his fist there long enough to choke the bastard! Blankenship gagged, then coughed, before writhing and kicking out in all directions at once.

Vince felt a sharp blow and intense pain as Blankenship kicked into his shin with the pointed toe of his cowboy boot. Every muscle in Vince's body groaned, then moved together as he willed himself upward in an adrenalin-fueled assault against Blankenship.

The two bodies flipped over. Now Blankenship lay with

his back against the pavement, Vince pressing down on top of him. He pushed Blankenship's face into the concrete with his own head and felt as much as heard the thud as Blankenship's cheekbone cracked against the pavement. Vince noticed, with some satisfaction, blood dripping from Blankenship's nose and already swollen left cheek.

But he still couldn't get to the gun. Vince clawed at Blankenship's chest trying to pry the gun from his hands. He heard the muffled click as the safety went off. He had to get the gun before Blankenship could pull the trigger!

Vince's thumbnail gouged deep into Blankenship's ribcage and he was able to get some traction on the gun's grip, beginning to wrestle it away from Blankenship's hold.

The third man finally snapped into action. He pulled Blankenship's arm straight out from his body with a single movement, scraping the downed man's elbow along the rough pavement as he did so. Blankenship cried out in pain. The Glock dropped to the cement and skittered in Lizzie's direction. She grabbed it and backed away from the trio that lay sprawled on the pavement.

Blankenship looked up, his mouth full of gravel and blood. He gave Vince one last kick and as Vince recoiled from the pain, Blankenship managed to pull himself free and stand up. He tripped on the jagged concrete and almost fell back down again.

For a few seconds, all four of them remained motionless, catching their breath in quick, deep gulps of smoky air. Then Blankenship shook his fist at them. "Motherfuckers! You'll be sorry!" He wiped the blood from his face and ran back to his car. He accelerated away from the junkyard without a backward glance.

The other man helped Vince to his feet. The three of them stood there, the only sounds their heavy breathing until the third explosion went off.

Then a low-pitched, blood-curdling howl rose from inside the metal shack.

# CHAPTER FIFTY-FOUR

"WHAT THE HELL was that?" Vince's heart sank to his toes. He knew exactly what it was: a dog, alone and terrified, somewhere in the smoke-filled lot. What kind of watchdog would hide as soon as anyone came on his property?

"Oh my god," Lizzie said. "I swear there wasn't a dog here before, just Rennie and all this junk. Shit. What are we going to do?"

Vince figured he'd find out in a second. The dog howled again, longer this time and higher pitched, insistent. The sound came from the only building standing on the property.

"I'm going in." He looked at Lizzie, who nodded, wild-eyed. She was still clutching the gun. Vince headed into the decrepit shack hoping like hell the dog had more sense than it had shown so far.

The smoke burned his eyes and he could barely see in the haze. His whole body throbbed with pain and he could still feel the bite of Blankenship's boot against his shin. By the time he saw the dog's silhouette in the darkness he was coughing and it hurt to breathe. The dog strained toward him. It was tied to an old tire and had moved as far as it could on the short lead. What the hell was wrong with people that they'd tie a dog up like this? No wonder the poor thing hadn't come outside when they first showed up.

"Okay, buddy." Vince tried to sound calm, reassuring. His voice shook. "We're gonna get you out of here." He reached toward the dog, wondering if it would try to take his arm off as he approached.

The dog was shaking. It didn't back away when Vince patted his head and crooned, "Good dog."

The dog was skinny, too skinny, and the studded collar slid right off its neck when Vince pushed it up and around its ears. "Let's go, buddy."

The dog wouldn't budge.

"Damn it! Come on!" The dog whimpered and lay down. Smoke was filling the space and Vince could barely see the dog lying right in front of him.

Vince leaned down. He felt no resistance as he picked the dog up. The dog was lighter than air, nothing but fur and bones. He could feel it trembling in his arms as he stumbled back toward the light. If only they could make it outside before his lungs burst.

He tripped.

He hit sharp metal on his way down and everything went dark.

When they heard Vince fall, Lizzie and the man Blankenship left behind raced into the shack. "Vince! Can you hear me?" Lizzie's voice was shrill.

Nothing.

By the time they reached him, the smoke was so dense they could just make out shapes by touch.

Arms, grabbing, pulling. Vince held tight to the dog, making it all the more difficult for Lizzie to grab hold of him. An eternity, or maybe only seconds, passed and the pile of arms and legs made it out of the building and to the concrete clearing.

Vince lay motionless, a trickle of blood oozing from his temple. His grip on the dog had loosened and Lizzie grabbed the dog, holding it tight against her chest.

Vince wasn't breathing.

"Give me some room. I'm gonna do CPR." The man in the Friends of the Wild T-shirt knelt down beside Vince. He tore Vince's shirt open and placed his hands, one on top of the other, in the middle of Vince's bare chest. He pushed hard and fast, again and again until, at last, Vince coughed and opened his eyes.

"Lizzie," he whispered and drifted back out of consciousness.

Friends of the Wild slapped Vince's face. "Wake up! You gotta stay awake!" Vince opened his eyes and moaned again.

Lizzie squeezed his hand, then wiped tears from her face and blood from his. "We've got to get out of here." She struggled to her feet, setting the dog down and trying to pull Vince up as she did so. The man grabbed Vince by the other arm and pulled until all of them were on their feet. "The car's right down the street," she said, pointing in the direction of her little red sedan.

They half-shuffled, half-ran toward the opening in the chain link fence. A woman, dressed in a pastel suit and high heels, stared at them as they passed her on the sidewalk. She said nothing, but scooped up the shivering dog and followed them.

By the time they got to the car, sirens were wailing in the distance. "Get in," Lizzie said between clenched teeth once they maneuvered Vince into the front seat.

She hit the gas. Five blocks later, screaming fire trucks passed them heading in the opposite direction.

# CHAPTER FIFTY-FIVE

LIZZIE GRIPPED THE steering wheel tight to keep from shaking. Vince breathed heavily on the seat beside her. No one spoke.

The plan that seemed merely implausible hours ago had, in the hard sharp light of Rennie's Scrap Metal, morphed into a complete and utter failure.

Lizzie slammed her hand against the steering wheel in frustration. She and Vince had been fools, both of them, so desperate to help Ernestine that they created a melodrama and a mess. Instead of saving her, all they'd managed to do was put her, and themselves, in greater jeopardy.

Lizzie's mind shifted back to the present when she glanced in the rearview mirror. She had passengers.

"Who the hell are you?" she turned back to look at the woman, still cradling the shaking dog. Black soot and dog snot were smeared across the front of her lavender suit jacket.

The woman's laugh came out sounding like a sob. "Oh my. What a mistake I made following y'all here. I'm

Doreen Loftus. You might recognize me as the Cake Lady. I have the *Cake Lady Show* on the Good Food Network. It's very popular. Do you watch it? We're syndicated throughout the country on more than a hundred stations. Here, let me get my card for you." She tried to reach her purse but the dog was sprawled across her lap.

"Well, now's probably not a good time for all that, I reckon." She laughed again. "I've been following your young man here," she patted Vince's shoulder and he moaned, "trying to get his burnt sugar filling recipe. I already promised it to my cookbook publisher, and I'm on deadline.

"I thought, come hell or high water, I'm getting that recipe today. You can't imagine how thrilled I was to see y'all pull out of your driveway this morning." She shifted the dog a bit. "I figured I'd just follow you until you stopped and I could talk to him. I never dreamed we'd end up out here. At the end of the world." She shuddered.

Lizzie cursed to herself. This woman had followed them for several hours and they hadn't noticed her. What else had they missed?

"I was so nervous about parking in that dreadful neighborhood I must have left the keys right there in the car, right there in the ignition. By the time I realized it–it was after those bombs started going off–I saw some young thugs drive off in it. I'm just glad it was a rental car and my publisher is paying."

She tried to wipe dog slobber off her suit. "This story will make it worth it, though. Maybe you would even like to be on the *Cake Lady Show* once you're feeling a little better." She patted Vince's shoulder again and he shifted away from her touch.

"Do you live in Moon Beach?" Lizzie asked.

"Oh, goodness gracious, no!" Doreen laughed. "I'm based in Atlanta."

Lizzie slowed the car and stopped next to an abandoned warehouse. Broken glass littered what was left of the sidewalk. They could still hear sirens in the distance. She turned and looked directly at the woman in the back seat. "Do you want to get home tonight?"

"What do you mean?"

"I mean, I can let you out of the car right here and now."

Doreen's eyes widened. "You wouldn't do that."

"No? As a matter of fact, I would." Lizzie paused to let that information sink in.

"Here's the deal. I can drop you off at the airport. We're pretty close. And then you will never, ever mention what happened today to anyone. Not one freaking word."

Doreen started to open her mouth.

"I'm not done yet. One word about being here, about meeting us, about Moon Beach, about the burnt sugar filling and we will press charges."

"Press charges? Whatever for?"

"Breaking and entering. You ransacked my dad's and Vince's kitchen looking for the damn recipe. Your fans wouldn't be too happy to learn that your cookbooks were full of stolen recipes, would they?"

"I didn't mean any harm. I just wanted that recipe and I couldn't figure out how to make anything that tasted nearly as good."

"That's because Vince is freaking brilliant and you're not. Now, are you getting out of the car here or what?

"I'd rather you dropped me off at the airport. Please."

Lizzie started the car again and drove to the airport. She pulled into the departing flights lane and stopped against the curb.

Lizzie grabbed Doreen's arm and forced her to make eye contact with her. "One more thing, Cake Lady. We have pictures," she lied.

"Pictures?"

"Yeah, surveillance camera pictures from the cottage. We just couldn't ID them before now. Since nothing seemed to be missing in the break-in, we didn't bother going to the police. But one word out of you and we will. Your cake lady career will be over." Lizzie grinned. "Have a nice flight."

Doreen got out of the car and tripped across the curb in her haste to get into the terminal.

Lizzie turned around to face her other passenger.

"Well?"

# CHAPTER FIFTY-SIX

PETER COULDN'T STOP shaking, even though they were miles away from Rennie's Scrap Metal. He was grateful for one thing: his grandmother's check supporting Green Eco-Tours was still in his pocket and not in Blankenship's bank account. To think he'd talked his own grandmother into giving money to that son of a bitch. How could he have been so stupid?

If he ever got back to South Dakota–and the way that lunatic was driving, he wasn't so sure–he'd apologize to Gram the second he got off the bus. Then he'd mow her lawn, take her to church, anything to try to make it up to her.

He felt sick to his stomach. Blankenship had just abandoned him at Rennie's to fend for himself. He could still be standing in that inferno trying to explain his presence to the cops. He'd have an arrest record instead of a research project to take home.

"Geez, thanks for not leaving me there in that hell hole. I really owe you. I'm Peter Cooper. I hate to admit it, but I was working with Mr. Blankenship."

"Lizzie here. And this is Vince." She put her hand on Vince's shoulder.

Vince groaned and opened his eyes. "Oh, man. Talk about a headache. What happened?"

"Hey, sunshine. Welcome back." Lizzie's voice shook.

"You scared us for a while there," Peter said. The dog squirmed out of his arms and over the seatback onto Vince's lap. It reached up and began licking Vince's face.

"It looks like you have a new best friend," Lizzie said. "Poor dog's nothing but a skeleton right now. Let's see how long that'll last on a diet of your lasagna and burnt sugar cannoli."

"Dogs are pretty smart." Peter leaned into the front seat to pat the dog. "They have good sense, better than most people. I'll bet he already knows you saved his life. He's not going to forget it."

The dog relaxed into Vince's arms. Vince groaned again. "Tell me I just had a bad dream. Tell me we didn't totally screw things up with Blankenship. We sure didn't do Ernestine any favors. We're lucky to be alive."

"Got that right." Lizzie looked at Peter in the rear view mirror. "How'd you get mixed up with a dipshit like Blankenship? Guy's an idiot."

"You don't even know the half of it," Peter said. "He's targeting rich people who want to say they've traveled up into the blackwater rivers where most tourists never go. So they could say they'd seen some bogus endangered species up close.

"He wants to run helicopters from some of the big resorts and have them land on the helipad he's planning to build on Moon Beach."

"Helipad?" Vince and Lizzie spoke in unison.

"Yeah, helipad." Peter's cheeks burned with shame and guilt. "From there, the tourists would go on guided kayak tours up through the wetlands and waterways. They'd spend an hour or so on the water and then have their pictures taken next to a lot of expensive equipment. They could fool their friends, and themselves, into thinking they were doing important ecological research.

"He fooled me too. Told me he got a special research exemption from the state to build the helipad. I was going to be the naturalist and head researcher, the kayak guide. It all sounded too good to be true. And I guess it was."

"Oh my god. A helipad. That's why he wants Ernestine's property," Lizzie said.

"Who's Ernestine?"

"Ernestine has lived in Moon Beach for like a zillion years and supported just about everyone here at one time or another. Blankenship is trying to grab her land," Lizzie said.

Vince turned to Peter. "This whole screwy plan you fell into at Rennie's was supposed to scare him enough to stop him. But I'm afraid all we did was piss him off."

"Mr. Blankenship can't get away with this," Peter said. "The guy doesn't even like nature. To him, green means money, nothing else. Bad enough for some of the big investors he conned, but for folks like my grandmother or Ernestine..." Peter's voice trailed off. "It just isn't fair to them."

"Got that right." Vince readjusted the dog in his lap. "Seeing Ernestine get screwed is what got us started. It didn't hurt that Blankenship is such an ass."

"What Peter's saying makes it even worse," Lizzie said. "It's not just Ernestine who's losing out, but all of Moon

Beach. Can you imagine that beautiful beach with freaking helicopters landing on it?

"It's going to take more than us and our stupid schemes to stop Blankenship. When he aimed that gun at me, his eyes were burning with hate. We're in his way, and he'll do whatever it takes to get rid of us." She choked back tears.

Peter felt the heavy weight of responsibility press down on him. While Lizzie and Vince had almost died trying to stop Blankenship, he'd been aiding and abetting the bastard.

He had to redeem himself. He just didn't know how.

Lizzie slowed down as they approached Moon Beach. "We're heading to the Whispering Pines Cottages. Can I drop you off somewhere first?"

"That'd be great." Peter gave her the name of a little apartment complex and she pulled into the parking lot a few minutes later. "Thanks for not leaving me at Rennie's."

"How could we? You just saved Vince's life."

Peter leaned over to Vince and said, "You better be careful for the next couple of days in case you hurt your head more than you thought. Like you should probably make sure to wake up every couple of hours at least tonight." He looked at Lizzie. "Can you do that? Wake him up a couple of times during the night?"

She nodded. "Of course."

Vince stared at her. She stared back.

"You can sleep on my couch. It's a pull-out. The dog'll love it."

# CHAPTER FIFTY-SEVEN

VINCE WALKED THE dog around the yard as soon as they got to Whispering Pines. It felt good to be back, even though his head was throbbing and every muscle ached.

Lizzie was pulling things out of the refrigerator when Vince walked indoors with the dog. "I'm starving," she said. "I'll bet the poor dog is, too. What are you gonna call him? He needs a name."

Vince sat down and the dog jumped on his lap. How could this animal be the same one he'd found cowering in the junkyard only hours earlier?

"Leroy. His name's Leroy. What do you think?" The dog perked his ears and wagged his tail.

"Leroy? How ironic," Lizzie said. "I'll bet this is one dog happy to give up his junkyard claim. He might even turn into a pussy cat."

Leroy licked Vince's face and then squirmed in closer to his chest. "You might be right. I think he's purring. Good boy, Leroy."

"I hope he likes scrambled eggs. You too. I'm tossing everything in them but the kitchen sink." She focused her attention on the large skillet in front of her.

Within minutes, the three of them devoured close to a dozen eggs, scrambled with cheese, ham, spinach, and tomato.

Lizzie put the empty plates on the floor for Leroy to lick clean.

"What kind of dog do you think Leroy is?"

"Beats me. Basic brown shepherd mix." Vince stroked the matted fur. "He'll be really something, though, after he has a bath and a couple weeks with enough to eat."

"Don't forget the most important part. Someone to love him." Lizzie's eyes widened into full moons as soon as she said it. She turned and looked away.

Vince felt a pull at his shoulder. He sat bolt upright in the dark. Where was he?

"Vince? It's me. I want to make sure you don't zone out too much. Like Peter said."

His eyes adjusted to the semi-darkness so he could see Lizzie kneeling beside the couch, frowning. "What's wrong?"

"I've been thinking about what could have happened today at Rennie's," she said. "You could be dead. We both could be dead. I'm just glad we're here. Alive."

"Me too."

Her hand was still on his shoulder when he drifted back to sleep. At least he hoped it was.

When Vince woke up again, it was to the smell of coffee and the sound of Lizzie humming. He smiled. If he had to get pummeled by Blankenship to wake up to that, it might just be worth the pain. Leroy wriggled with excitement as soon as Vince sat up.

"Coffee?" She'd already poured him a mug. "Hey, you look even worse in daylight than you did last night." She pointed to a fragrant platter on the table. "We're in luck. I found a bunch of your cinnamon rolls stashed in the freezer, so I warmed them up. Dig in." She took a big bite and licked her lips.

"Leroy seems to have settled in okay." The dog looked up when Lizzie said his name. "I can't believe Rennie just tied the poor thing in the shed like that."

"Do you think he'll miss the dog?"

"He sure didn't take very good care of him," Lizzie said. "Who knows the last time he'd even fed Leroy."

"We screwed up almost everything yesterday. But we might have saved Leroy's life by showing up at Rennie's," Vince said.

"You think the whole fiasco was worth it?"

"Maybe parts of it were." Vince toyed with his coffee. He couldn't quite figure out how or why, but he knew he was a different person than he'd been twenty-four hours earlier.

The doorbell rang. Leroy cocked his ear toward the door for an instant before settling back down in the chair.

"Some watchdog we got here, huh?" Vince scratched the dog's neck and walked to the door.

Peter Cooper was standing on the front steps of Lizzie's cottage. A bicycle leaned against the porch railing.

"I just wanted to check and see how you were doing after the pounding you went through yesterday," Peter said when he walked in. He reached into his day pack and pulled out a bag of dog food. "I rode by the grocery store on my way here and got this for the dog."

He looked at the pull-out couch, then at both Lizzie

and Vince. "Hey, I didn't mean to throw you guys together for the night. I thought—"

Lizzie's cheeks were scarlet.

"Well, it doesn't matter what I thought. I saw your car out front and figured I'd find you here. I wanted to thank you both for yesterday," Peter said.

"For what? We messed up pretty bad," Vince said.

"Maybe so, but you knocked some sense into my head. There I was, helping that idiot ruin the coast. And there you were, risking your lives to save a friend. I didn't like myself much in the comparison."

He sat down and Lizzie poured him some coffee. He looked at the cinnamon rolls. "Those smell delicious."

"Help yourself. They're one of Vince's many specialties."

Peter ate two rolls before speaking again. "I'm heading back home to South Dakota. Just gotta tie up some loose ends first, try to make amends. Thanks for shaking me up."

"You saved my life," Vince said. "I owe you big time."

"In some ways you guys saved my life, too. If I'd stuck with Blankenship..." Peter's voice trailed off and he shook his head.

"I wish we could stop him," Lizzie said.

"Maybe only Blankenship himself can do that," Peter said. "If he destroys the coast and pisses enough people off, eventually he'll dig his own grave."

"If he's gonna dig his own grave, let's hope he does it before he builds a blasted helipad," Lizzie said.

# CHAPTER FIFTY-EIGHT

PETER WALKED INTO Words & More. Vince and Lizzie had been right. The bookstore was worth a visit. He headed to the local interest section and started pulling books from the shelf.

"May I help you?"

He turned toward the voice. That must be Anne. Already he had picked out a small pile of books about the region.

"Maybe." He smiled and stuck out his hand. "I'm Peter Cooper. I, um, met your friends Vince and Lizzie and they told me about you and your bookstore. I wanted to come in before heading back home. And pick up some books about the area."

"You chose some good ones. Back home?"

"Yeah. South Dakota. I've already got my bus ticket. I've been here on a college internship. I wish I'd met folks like Vince and Lizzie earlier instead of the ones I did meet up with," he said. "You could help me with something."

"I'd be happy to. What can I do for you?"

"Well, I'd like to take home a couple of books for my

grandmother. Something she might really enjoy. Any suggestions?"

"Some ladies from the Senior Center were in a couple of days ago and I can show you the books they bought."

"That'd be awesome."

"Maybe, maybe not. Wait a second and I'll get them." Two minutes later Anne walked back carrying the erotic trilogy and the thrillers.

Peter's face turned bright red when he saw the steamy covers. "Oh wow. This isn't exactly what I was expecting."

"I'll bet."

"What the hell. I'll take all of them. I'm dying to see her face when she opens the package. Thanks."

Anne rang up the sales and put the books in a bag. "I hope you've had a chance to explore the area a little bit. It's really beautiful."

"It sure is. I just hope it can stay that way."

# CHAPTER FIFTY-NINE

PETER YANKED OPEN the door to the Green Eco-Tours office. Blankenship bolted up at his desk, startled. "Don't you know how to knock, boy?"

Peter ignored the slight. "You're coming for a ride with me."

Blankenship laughed. "I don't think so."

His eyes widened when he saw Peter's right hand. "We picked up your gun after you dropped it," Peter said. "It's still loaded. Let's go."

Peter pointed the gun directly at Blankenship's chest. Blankenship stood up slowly.

"You drive," Peter directed when they were on the sidewalk. "I'll tell you where to go."

Fifteen minutes later they pulled up to a decrepit boat ramp not far from Ernestine's cottage. Two kayaks were moored to the ramp.

"Get in the green kayak," Peter said.

Blankenship didn't budge.

"Watch this." Peter grabbed the keys and got out of the car. He aimed the Glock at a buoy marker in the water.

There was a sharp *ping* as the bullet hit the buoy marker dead center. "My dad started taking me hunting when I was nine. I'm a really good shot. Now get out of the car."

Blankenship got out and started limping down the boat ramp. His alligator cowboy boots hit the warped boards with a heavy clink at each step.

"Get in and start paddling." Blankenship looked at the gun, then slowly lowered himself into the kayak. Peter handed him a paddle and pushed the kayak into the current, then stepped easily into the second kayak.

The tide was coming in and the kayaks were able to glide inland with the tide and practically no effort from either paddler.

After twenty minutes of paddling and drifting, the water around the kayaks was dark with tannin. Cypress trees clung to the shoreline. There was no sound beyond the paddles hitting the water, no sign that civilization had preceded them here.

"Pull over here." Peter steered the kayaks into a hidden cove between cypress knees and a fallen tree. He drew a Green Eco-Tours brochure from his pocket and started reading aloud:

*In the lush tidal backwaters untouched by human development, you will be able to see and hear those wild creatures that only a few are fortunate enough to experience. You may see herons gliding through the cathedral-like arches formed by the overhanging cypress, dipping down into the dark water to snag a fish. The dark water itself is home to many species, and we urge you to use caution as the waters are alive with both beauty and danger. What looks like a bobbing log may be an alligator. What looks like a pile of rotting leaves could be a coiled cottonmouth waiting to strike.*

*This is a journey not for the faint of heart, but for the passionate ecotourist willing to put his life on the line for a glimpse of the world unseen by most and available only to the privileged few.*

Peter looked up from the brochure. He noticed sweat stains growing around Blankenship's armpits. "Heard enough?" He grabbed Blankenship's paddle and threw it into his own kayak.

"What the hell are you doing?"

"This is what's known as being up shit creek without a paddle, Mr. Blankenship. If you're patient and stay in the kayak, the tide'll begin to roll out in about an hour. You should be able to roll out with it then," Peter said.

"Until then, you might want to use the time to think about your plans to ravage this beautiful place. And what you might want to do instead of spoiling paradise. If I were you, I wouldn't step out into the water here. Beauty and danger and all that."

Peter maneuvered his own kayak back into the main part of the stream and used powerful movements to distance himself from Blankenship and his own bad decisions as he headed back to the boat ramp.

He threw the Glock overboard in the black water, hoping salt and sand would work together to make it useless should anyone find it.

He'd had it with the entire coastal region. It was beautiful here, but people like Blankenship were more than eager to spoil it. And there were too many ways they could.

All Peter could think about now was getting home.

Blankenship watched Peter's kayak glide around a bend and disappear. The sound of the paddle dipping into the water receded into the distance. Tiny flies swarmed around his head and landed on every bit of exposed skin. He slapped at them, but the movement only seemed to encourage more insects to attack.

A heavy shroud of silence engulfed him. He looked at his watch. He'd been here, alone, for four minutes. He looked up at the trees, towering menacingly above him. No way could he last until the tide turned and ran back out to the coast and civilization.

Seven minutes. Blankenship could feel his face and arms swelling from bug bites. He wiped sweat off his face with his palm and came away with a handful of dead no-see-ems.

Nine minutes. Fuck it. He'd push the goddamned kayak back downstream himself if that's what it would take to get out of this hell hole right now.

He stepped gingerly out of the kayak and into the dark stream.

A slight ripple danced in the water along the opposite bank.

# CHAPTER SIXTY

BY LATE AFTERNOON Vince was feeling antsy and uncomfortable. Being here in Lizzie's little cottage with her felt so right it scared him. But he was in the way, he had to be in that small space. Vince swore he could feel the air current move each time Lizzie breathed in, breathed out. His own breath fell into a rhythm with hers and that soothed him. But not enough to untangle the web of thoughts whirling through his brain.

He was conscious of the sun hitting her long legs, conscious of the pattern of freckles on her left arm, conscious of his own inability to speak. Finally he stood up, with no idea where he would go from there.

Lizzie looked at him. "You feel up for a walk on the beach? It'd probably do you good to get some fresh air and clear out your lungs. We could walk down to Ernestine's. Maybe even catch the sunset. I'll bet Leroy's never been to the beach."

Getting outdoors would be a relief. He hoped.

Leroy pranced down the wooden walkway to the beach as if he'd been walking there every day of his life. When they got to the sparkling expanse of sand, Leroy raced ahead, barking at the shorebirds along the waterline. He chased after the birds as they flew up just a few feet out of his reach.

"Looks like he's getting into his new life pretty fast," Vince said. Leroy looked nothing like the shivering pile of fur and bones Vince had found cowering in the shack at Rennie's. For an instant Vince saw Lizzie standing in the junkyard with Blankenship pointing a gun at her. A wave of cold fear washed over him.

"Oh my god." The words were out before Vince realized he'd spoken out loud.

"What?"

"I was thinking about Blankenship." That wasn't quite true: he was thinking about Lizzie. Thinking about not being able to move fast enough to save her. Thinking about what he would have done if she'd been hurt, or worse.

Thinking about what he wanted to say to her.

Instead he said, "I'm sorry I dragged you into that mess." That wasn't true either. He'd been glad Lizzie was there with him. Especially since they'd lived through it.

Was he imagining that she looked disappointed by what he said?

Lizzie shrugged. "Eh. Parts of it were fun. I wish we'd been able to scare Blankenship though."

They walked along the beach silently. Vince was acutely aware of each breath Lizzie took, waiting to see if she would speak. Waiting to see if he would.

"When I saw him pointing that gun at you..." Vince stopped. How could he tell her?

"Hey, look at Leroy. He's really getting into playing in

the water." Lizzie pointed down the beach.

Leroy raced along the water's edge, chasing the ribbon of foam that rippled down the beach as each incoming wave hit the shoreline. He paid no attention to the sandpipers running alongside him in the foam, digging their beaks into the wet sand for tiny mollusks.

A school of minnows flashed silver against a breaking wave and Leroy leaped in the water to chase after the shimmering fish. When the wave splashed over him, the dog jumped back in surprise. Lizzie and Vince laughed.

"This sure beats Rennie's, huh Leroy?" But the dog was too intent on running along the beach to hear Vince.

"Looks like he's going to run all the way down to Ernestine's." They watched as Leroy raced down the beach and waded into the tidal stream near Ernestine's cottage. He poked at a dark patch in the water until he wrestled something loose and grabbed it in his teeth.

"I think he found something to play with," Vince said as the dog tossed his new treasure up in the air, catching it on the way down.

"Leroy! Come here!" Leroy tossed the toy up once more, caught it and ran back to Vince and Lizzie. He dropped the wet object at Vince's feet.

"Leroy found part of a shoe," Vince said.

"It looks more like a boot to me, a cowboy boot. Look at the tooling on that thing." Lizzie pointed to the intricate leatherwork. "Blankenship's the only fool I know who'd wear fancy cowboy boots like that at the beach, but I'll bet there are a boatload of others."

Vince knelt down to examine the piece of leather more closely. "That jagged edge," he said as he picked it up. "Looks like teeth marks."

"Sure does. Almost like a gator took a chunk out of it."
Lizzie giggled. "And then spit it out when he realized it
was kin."

"Good score, Leroy. Go see what else you can find."
Vince tossed the piece of alligator leather back to Leroy.
The dog pranced off, still carrying the piece of boot in his
mouth. He headed back toward Ernestine's and the tidal
stream.

Vince took a deep breath and picked a shell up from
the sandy beach. He handed it to Lizzie.

"What's this?" She turned the little purple and white
shell over in her hand and rubbed its smooth surface.

"The first morning your dad and I were in Whispering
Pines, I walked down here to the beach and bam, right off
I met Ernestine. She gave me a shell like this and told me
to hold on to it. It was all part of the Moon Beach magic,
she said. I thought she was talking some kind of mumbo-
jumbo, but I kept the shell for good luck anyway.

"I didn't know what she meant back then, but I do
now. She was absolutely right. There is magic. Right here.
Right in front of my eyes."

A line of pelicans glided inches above the water and
seagrass waved in the breeze along the dunes. Sunlight
reflected off Lizzie's hair as soft strands of copper blew
across Vince's face.

"Lizzie."

She turned to face him, smiling. Slowly he ran his
fingers through her hair, gathering it gently away from her
face, letting his hands touch first the back of her head,
then the back of her neck. His hands trembled as he
traced the outline of her lips, felt their moist heat radiating
out to his fingertips.

She moaned his name softly and slid her hands to his shoulders, then around to the back of his neck. He wrapped his arms around her, pulling her close to him.

Finally their lips touched.

This time, the fireworks were real. And very, very close.

## ABOUT THE AUTHOR

Natasha Alexander lives and dreams along the southeastern coast of the United States. She writes contemporary fiction featuring quirky characters stumbling toward self-awareness, decent cannoli, and possibly love. *Moon Beach Magic* is her first novel. She is currently writing a mystery, tentatively titled *Pelican Island*.

In earlier lifetimes, Natasha worked in publishing, taught at varying levels from kindergarten through university, designed interactive video, attended theological school, and conducted ethnographic research in urban schools around the country. Not all at the same time, though.

If she's not writing, she's probably walking on the beach or singing. Occasionally both at the same time.

Please visit Natasha online at her website.

http://natasha.edcentric.org/

9759190R00144

Made in the USA
San Bernardino, CA
27 March 2014